Timeless

A Novella by Erin Noelle

Timeless

Published by Erin Noelle

Cover design by Hang Le

Cover photo by Mighty Aphrodite Photography

Editing by Kayla Robichaux

Formatting by Kassi Cooper

For Nicki, Trina,

Kirsten, and MJ

Before the beta-reading, before the covers,
before the stress of hitting the 'publish' button,
and before everything else that goes along
with this crazy world we've embarked upon,
you ladies were there. I wouldn't be here
without every one of you. There are no words
to express my appreciation and love.

Contents

The Wedding

(Come to Me ~ The Goo Goo Dolls)

SCARLETT

One thing I've learned about life in my short time here is that it never goes as planned. Getting up each time it knocks you down is hard; some of us get knocked down more than others, but in my opinion, we're the ones that are stronger in the end. After Ash died, I truly thought I'd never love anyone again. Even after I'd come to terms with all of it and began to love myself for me, I didn't think I could make myself susceptible to feeling pain like that again. But when Mase showed up on my door step that morning, all of that went out the window. I realized that loving yourself is vital because then, and only then, do you realize you deserve the love of another.

I'd love to say he walked in that day, swept me off my feet again, and we rode off into the sunset happily ever after, but that isn't reality, and actually it isn't even the ending of most books anymore.

"Mommy, Auntie Andi says it's time for us to get married," a sweet, tiny voice interrupts my thoughts.

I turn around to see my precious daughter standing in the doorway, dressed in her light pink sundress and flip flops. Laughing, I walk over to her and pick her up. "Did Auntie Andi say that you can get married in those shoes?" She nods her head with a big grin on her face. “Well, in that case, I'm wearing my flip flops too. You don't think Daddy will mind do you?”

“No, Daddy and Everett have on their new black Chucks. He said you'd like them,” she says with a giggle.

I roll my eyes as I set Ashlynn down on the ground. “I don't care what they wear, as long as we all get to get married.” I bend down to kiss the top of her head. “Now go tell Auntie Andi that Mommy will be there in five minutes.”

As she takes off down the hallway, I spin around to look at myself one last time in the mirror, taking a deep breath. Mase and I didn't get to this point the conventional way, and I wouldn't necessarily recommend it to anyone else, but it is how our book had to be written in order to get the ending just right.

The wedding ceremony is perfect - even with Ashlynn announcing her need to pee in the middle of the vows - and the reception is even better. I couldn't stop smiling as I witness our friends and family eating, dancing, and having an overall great time. As the evening comes to an end, Mase comes up to me and grabs my hand. “I've got a surprise for you.”

He leads me and all of the guests outside, then walks over to the event coordinator and whispers something in her ear. Returning to me, he stands behind me and circles his arms around my waist, pulling my back close to his chest. A song begins playing through the outside speakers and he starts singing lowly into my ear. Then suddenly, the sky fills with butterflies - thousands of them. I stand there in complete awe, looking up into the heavens as the beautiful creatures blanket the sky.

He continues his serenade “Come to me my sweetest friend, this is where we start again...” When the song was over, he turns me around in his arms and presses his forehead to mine. “Scarlett Alexandria Templeton, I have finally found my euphoria.”

Chapter One

MOVING DAY

(Lego House ~ Ed Sheeran)

SCARLETT

Collapsing on the cool, hardwood floor of our new living room, I close my eyes and press my overheated cheek against the smooth surface, silently wishing it was a week into the future. Hopefully then, this place would be unpacked, organized, and somewhat decorated. Forcing my lids open, I peer at the sea of boxes and storage containers surrounding my limp, exhausted body. As I scan the room, mentally assessing the damage, my gaze lands on two black Chucks in the pathway leading to the front foyer, one of the toes tapping. I can't help but smile, knowing that shoe holds a small part of a body I've grown to love so much. Automatically, my eyes lustfully journey upwards, traveling first over the long, denim-covered legs, then across the Sublime t-shirt plastered with sweat against the toned torso. I finally reach the face that stars in both my sweetest and naughtiest dreams—my husband.

My husband, I repeat the words in my head, still somewhat in disbelief we've made it to this point.

"Scarlett Alexandria Templeton, what in the world are you doing?" His attempt to scold me is unsuccessful as the edges of his lips curl up in a cheeky grin.

Rolling over onto my back, I move my arms and legs back and forth, making angels in the pretend-snow. "I'm being the angel you always tell me I am," I reply deadpan. "This is my role in the marriage, right?"

In the blink of an eye, he's on top of me—his damp, sticky body blanketing mine while he tickles my sides relentlessly. Wiggling, squirming, and flopping like a fish out of water, I try desperately to escape his grasp, but to no avail. Straddling my hips, his weight keeps the lower-half of my body prisoner as he manages to somehow pin both of my wrists to the floor above my head with only one of his hands, leaving his other hand free to taunt and tease the most sensitive areas of my body.

"Stop it! Please! I'm sorry!" I frantically plead in-between my gasps for air.

"Nope," he says with a wicked laugh. "You wanted to be funny, now I'm showing you how funny I can be."

For what seems like hours—but is actually only a few minutes—he tortures me with those five fingers, alternating from my ribcage, to my waist, to under my chin. All I can do is lie there with my eyes closed and pray I don't pee in my pants. Eventually, his movements grow slower and the frantic motion is replaced with a light stroking of his hands across the bare skin of my stomach. I open my eyes to look up at his scruffy but still extremely handsome face, and the playful, mischievous look in his steel-colored irises has morphed into a lustful hunger. Without thought, my body reacts, my hips lifting up and pressing into him as my core floods with desire.

"What are you doing?" he asks, feigning innocence, his stare glued to my chest as he pushes my cotton tank top further up to expose my pale pink bra.

"What are *you* doing?" I respond breathily, now unashamedly grinding against his crotch.

His fingertips lazily trail along the edge of my demi-cup, coming ever-so-close to my hardening nipples straining to be freed. "I'm trying to remind my wife that we have lots of things we're supposed to be doing, and napping on the living room floor isn't one of them."

Moaning softly, my back bows up off the ground, arching into his caress. Like a skilled snake charmer, his touch is my pungi, hypnotizing my body to slink and sway in an erotic dance of passion. I'm his willing captive, his adored angel, his loving wife. But most of all, I'm just *his*.

"I think I need more reminding," I whisper. I'm fully aware we're both a sweaty mess, but I couldn't care less. With what I have in mind, we'll just get sweatier and messier.

Tearing his heavy-lidded eyes from my breasts, he moves his gaze up to meet mine, flashing me a wicked grin. "You promise you'll be productive afterwards?" He pushes his rock-hard cock down and rotates his hips slightly against my throbbing clit as he asks.

"Mhmm," I groan, tilting my head back, offering the delicate skin of my neck to him. "I promise I'll be good."

He lowers his face to mine, and his lips hover so close I can almost taste him. Instead of feeding my hunger for his kiss, he dips down and traces his nose along my jawline—chin to ear, and back again—as his thumb dips under the satin fabric, flicking my pebbled nipple. "I never said anything about being good," he mumbles, peppering kisses down my throat and across my collarbone.

I attempt to free my hands from his hold; I want to touch him...I *need* to touch him. The fiery ache seeded deep in my belly blazes through my body from the tingles in my scalp, down to the sizzling sensation in my toes, all converging in sweltering chaos between my legs. "Please, Mase," I beg, "I'm gonna be a worthless mess if you don't finish this now."

Laughing softly, he lifts his chest up and looks down at me. "The movers will be back in about twenty minutes. What if they walk in and see us?"

"We can be fast," I reply quickly, still squirming underneath him. We have five-year-old twins; we've mastered the act of fast sex.

He leans down and captures my mouth with his in a greedy, demanding kiss. He never denies me what I want, especially when what I want is him buried deep inside of me. "Stand up. Shorts and panties around your ankles. Bend over those boxes." His bossiness enthralls me, my body and mind always eager to please him.

Hopping to his feet, he helps me up off the floor and I hurriedly obey his commands. My frayed denim cutoffs and pink striped panties slide effortlessly down my legs. Locating a stack of boxes at the perfect height, I bend at the waist and rest my chest on top of the flat, cardboard surface with the word *BOOKS* scribbled in black permanent marker across it. I chuckle to myself, thinking I not only read about sex in books, I now have sex *on top of* books.

He wastes no time giving me exactly what I want. As soon as I hear the zipper and the sound of clothes rumpling behind me, the tip of his erection slides up and down my slippery folds twice before he plunges deep inside of me. Bracing myself for the ride, he grabs my hips and begins to thrust in and out at the perfect pace. Over our years together, we've both learned how to play each other's bodies like fine-tuned instruments. Even though we're both skilled musicians, there's nothing more harmonious than the sounds we make when our bodies move together—no matter if we're tenderly making love, or fucking each other's brains out.

Looking at him over my shoulder, I thoroughly enjoy watching him claim my body time and time again. The flexing of his inked arms with each thrust. The way he unconsciously sucks on his lip ring. The darkening of his eyes to a charcoal gray as he climbs closer to his orgasm. Every expression entrancing, every movement mesmerizing.

He digs his thumbs into the dimples nestled at the small of my back, and I know the end is near. His eyes are locked on mine as he pounds into me, each stroke pushing me higher and higher to the peak of ecstasy. One final plunge and we both freefall together as the white-hot flames coursing through my veins deliver an all-encompassing rapture. Absolute perfection.

Collapsing on top of me, his stomach flush against my back, he kisses the feather tattoo on my left shoulder blade peeking out from the spaghetti strap of my shirt. Neither of us moves for several minutes, until our ragged breathing returns to normal and our pulse stabilizes. Eventually, he slowly slides out of me, and I whimper softly at his absence.

Chuckling, he slaps my naked ass and steps back to pull up his boxers and jeans. "You're insatiable, *woman*! Now get dressed and get to unpacking all these boxes like you promised," he teases. "If you're lucky, I'll reward you later for your hard work."

"Whatever, *man*. We've got three days with no kids, and I fully plan on taking advantage of our time alone." I playfully roll my eyes as I redress, adding quietly, "Boxes...shmoxes."

He silences my grumblings with an affectionate kiss. "I love you, Scarlett. I'm so glad we're here—in our own home. We're finally doing it right."

"I love you too, Mase," I reply, beaming back at him.

Our moment is interrupted by a knock at the door; the movers have returned with the final load of furniture. Quickly kissing me one more time, he goes to let them in and assist in getting everything in the correct room. As I spin around slowly, trying to decide where to start, a container in the corner labeled *PHOTOS* catches my eye. I know this is at the bottom of the priority list, but curiosity gets the best of me. Dragging it into the middle of the room, I pop open the side locks, anxious to find out what's inside.

Chapter Two

HOMECOMING

(You're the Reason I Come Home ~ Ron Pope)

SCARLETT

The first picture waiting when I open the treasure chest of memories is one of Mason, Max, and me the night of the Jobu's Rum homecoming party at Empty's Pub. Even though we all appear to be genuinely happy, a different expression plays on the face of each of us. Max appears to be giddy and spirited with his flushed cheeks, Mase looks relieved and appreciative, and I...well, a glimmer of hope and promise sparkles in my mossy-green eyes.

Grabbing the next few photos on the top of the pile—all from the same night—there's one of the entire band doing shots of tequila, another of me with my acoustic on stage, and finally, one of me and Mase locked in a passionate kiss. It was a night I'll never forget—the night our love was resurrected.

After Mason showed up at my apartment, returning the bracelet to me with the addition of the Psyche butterfly charm, I didn't see him for a couple of weeks. We spoke on the phone and texted often, but I was more than a bit overwhelmed with his unannounced arrival and the information about him getting daily reports on my healing process. Understanding and supportive, he kept his distance at my request, not wanting to pressure me into anything, but always reminding me he was there. I think I had three or four therapy sessions with Heather in the week following, as I struggled to surface under the multitude of emotions drowning me. Joy. Sorrow. Love. Guilt. Excitement. Optimism. Love. Grief. Forgiveness. Love. The one sentiment I always came back to was love—my love for Ash, my love for Mason.

When Max first told me about the big party Marcus was throwing for the band's homecoming from their first world tour, I had no intentions of going. I hadn't been in Empty's since I left for California with Ash. Its walls held too many memories, and I was afraid if I ever returned, they would ruthlessly throw them in my face. But as the day drew closer, my love for Mason became more and more palpable, and I realized I was unable to break free from the hold he had on my heart. I knew what I needed to do.

No one except for Max and Andi knew I was coming, not even Mina. Thankfully, the clear January night offered colder-than-usual temperatures, so I was able to conceal myself inside a heavy parka and scarf as I walked through the front door of the bar I'd spent so many of my nights in. Working my way through the body-to-body crowd, I may have been able to hide from the people, but I couldn't escape the pungent aroma of beer flowing freely from the taps, the vibrations from the live music reverberating throughout my body, the hum in the atmosphere thick with whispers of sex and lust, and all of the memories accompanying the devastatingly familiar sensations.

Immediately, I knew exactly where Mase was; all I had to do was locate the hoard of scantily-clad females and I could see the top of his recently-buzzed head directly in the center. Staying close to the outer wall, I made my way over to 32 Leaves' table, where Max and Andi were sitting. As soon as they saw me, both of them hurried over to me, making sure I was ready to go with everything. Unsure if I was more nervous or excited, the exhilaration pumped through me either way.

"You sure you're ready for this?" Max asked, true concern for my wellbeing evident in his voice.

Nodding, I smiled modestly at him. "It's time. I have to move on; as hard as it is, I have to keep on living. He would want that."

He pulled me into a tight embrace, kissing my cheek. "You're gonna be great, Scarlett. The acoustic's waiting for you on the side of the stage. I'll make sure the mic is on."

Before I could talk myself out of it, I stripped out of my outerwear and made my way towards the stage. Grabbing the guitar, I jumped up on the elevated surface, anxiety twisting in my stomach. Several people took notice of my presence immediately, but it wasn't until I tapped lightly on the microphone that I got the attention of the entire room.

Laughing nervously, I glanced over to the area of the Jobu's Rum table. "This feels like déjà vu. I'm almost positive I've stood in this exact same spot, telling the exact same man I want to give it another shot." I paused briefly to clear my throat, praying the moisture would return to my parched mouth. "I know everyone's here tonight to welcome our very own Jobu's Rum back home, and even though I'm thrilled to see Cruz, Aaron, and Sebastian again, this song is for the only Rummer that owns my heart."

I'd thought long and hard about what song I wanted to perform that night. There were so many options in which the lyrics nailed my feelings for Mase on the head, but no song had more meaning than Avril Lavigne's "I Love You"—the song he sang to me at Mina and Noah's wedding. As soon as I began the opening chords of my acoustic version, my eyes found his, and magically, every other person in the bar morphed into a blurry version of themselves. They were merely background scenery for the moment. Our moment. Somehow, I made it through the entire song without shedding a tear, but after I sang my last "La la la, that's why I love you," I lowered the guitar to rest on the floor, and said to him, "Consider my wings clipped, Mase." And then, the water works began.

Instantly, I was engulfed in his arms, deafened by the cheers and applause surrounding us. Then we were kissing—kissing like no one else was there. Mouths devouring. Hands roaming. Lips claiming. Tongues coaxing. Hearts submitting.

And thus, our love was reborn.

"Scarlett, come in here, please." Mason's voice echoes through the house, ripping me from my blissful reminiscence. "We need to know where you want the bed."

Startled, I hop to my feet and head towards the master bedroom, where he and the movers await my instructions for furniture placement. Once we get all of the pieces in just the right spots, Mase runs back outside to help the movers bring in the kids' furniture. Hoping it will take them a while to get it unloaded and up the stairs, I scurry back over to the container of old pictures, eager to see what else I can find.

Chapter Three

Moving On and Moving In

(Come On Get Higher ~ Matt Nathanson)

SCARLETT

Plopping back down on the floor next to the container of old photos, I open several additional boxes and set a few miscellaneous items out around me, in an attempt to appear productive. I dig back into the pictures and pull out another handful, excited for my next journey down Memory Lane. On top of the stack, I find myself staring into familiar green eyes sparkling with excitement and wonder, a young woman ready to embark on an expedition of the unknown. Flipping through a few more, there are shots of me and Mase, the entire band, me and Sophie, and a few of all six of us together. We're all standing next to the tour bus—which we later nicknamed *Cerrano*—the day I left to go on tour with Jobu's Rum.

After the band returned from their first tour, they all moved back to Houston to record their second album, claiming they no longer needed to be in Austin since they'd been discovered. I always wondered how much Mason had to do with the decision, but I never asked. We began to date, taking things as slowly as possible, which is easier said than done once you've already lived and been intimate with said person. However, I was afraid if we jumped back in at full throttle, we'd ultimately have the same ending as before.

I continued my individual therapy sessions with Heather, as did Mase, but we began seeing her as a couple too. To most people, a couple needing therapy in the dating stage of their relationship seems strange and destined for failure, but with our history and the grief I was still recovering from, it was crucial to have a solid foundation upon which to build a healthy relationship. Both of us quickly realized we had to let go of the 'what ifs' and 'what would've happeneds' if there was any chance for us. What if he would've asked me to move to Austin with him? What if Bentley wouldn't have answered the phone? What would've happened if I didn't sleep with Max? What if he would've died when he overdosed? What would've happened if I never came to see him at rehab? What if I didn't go to Vegas to see his concert? What if Ash hadn't died? *Too many questions and no definite answers. Letting go of the past was our biggest obstacle, but we were both determined to give 'us' a real chance, and that was the only way.*

Jobu's Rum wrapped up their recording sessions roughly three weeks before they headed out on their second domestic tour, this one lasting about eight months. Mason and I had been seeing each other again for a little over four months, but our time together was limited, due to his countless hours in the studio. To celebrate the completion of the album, he and I took off for a long weekend of relaxation and rejuvenation at The Hotel Galvez on Galveston beach. Heartrending and bittersweet yet breathtakingly perfect, the weekend marked a huge milestone in my healing process.

Tasting the salty sea breeze each time I inhaled, memories of Ash flooded my mind, mimicking the fierce surf crashing around my bare feet buried in the sandy shore. I stood frozen, lost in my thoughts for a long while; Mason respectfully hung back on the beach, allowing me as much time as I needed to say yet another round of goodbyes. When the tide changed and began to roll back out to the gulf, an odd sensation swept over me, leaving goose bumps from head to toe. As the waves stripped away layers of coastline, much of the guilt and sorrow I'd continued to harbor began to wash away as well. I'd never been one to believe in angels and spirits, but in that moment, I could've sworn Ash was there with me, telling me it was time to let go and move on, relieving me from the responsibility I felt.

That weekend was the first time Mase and I made love since reuniting. Never before had he been so tender and attentive, both of us recognizing the significance of the experience, almost as if we were both putting the past to rest and focusing on our future together. The following morning at breakfast, he asked me to go on tour with him, claiming he couldn't bear the thought of being without me for eight months. Thinking out all of my possible arguments beforehand, he maintained I had no real obligations keeping me in Houston—I hadn't gone back to college since I moved back from California, my job in the music room at the neighborhood center could easily be filled, and Andi was at my and Max's apartment nearly all the time anyhow, so it made sense for her to move in there, and for me to move in with Mase. He reasoned if I was as all-in on the relationship as he was, touring would be a part of his foreseeable future, so we might as well learn how to live on a bus together. The thought of him being gone had been nagging at me as well, and truth be told, it was one of the main reasons I was hesitant to become serious with him again. There was no point in getting attached if he was going to leave again.

Naturally, I was thrilled when he asked, especially with the newfound solace and serenity I felt; however, before I could say yes, I had a few people I needed to talk to first. The following week, I went to visit Robin, Ash's mom—who I'd stayed close with since everything had happened—and we called his sister, Crys, while I was there so I could discuss the situation with both of them simultaneously. With overwhelming reassurance from both of them, I began making plans to leave with Mase and the band.

Fast forward two weeks and I'm standing in the parking lot next to the bus, saying my goodbyes to Max, Andi, and Mina as they all wished us well and safe travels. The heat from the early-June sun was only amplified as it bounced off of the dark pavement, but I couldn't tell if it was that or the nerves buzzing wildly through me that had my cheeks flushing a rosy pink.

"Are you ready to be famous?" Andi asked as she took my picture with her phone.

Rolling my eyes, I shook my head at her. "I'm not going to be famous, silly. It's just these guys. Sophie and I will have the high honor of cleaning up after them, and throwing annoying groupies off the bus. Right, Soph?" I said as I beckoned Aaron's wife over to the conversation.

Strolling over to us, she threw her arm around my shoulders and gave me a squeeze. "You have no idea, my dear friend. I hope you brought your suit of armor, 'cause you're gonna need it," she warned yet again.

Ever since Sophie found out I was going with them, she and I had started hanging out more. She was excited to have another female on the bus, but told me from the beginning she wasn't going to sugar-coat things for me; the first tour almost broke apart her and Aaron's four-year relationship. I had a good idea what I was in for, and had tried my best to prepare myself for it. I figured after all Mase and I had been through, if we couldn't manage to make it through this, then maybe it just wasn't meant to be.

After a final round of hugs and photos with everyone, the six of us boarded the oversized, jet-black bus, along with the driver, Ed, and their new agent/ promoter, Owen, who I absolutely adored, especially compared to his predecessors. The first few hours on the road we spent unpacking and acquainting ourselves with where everything was on the pre-stocked apartment-on-wheels. I was floored with how homey and spacious everything seemed at first. Little did I know how rapidly that feeling would dissipate.

We spent the first few days traveling to Vegas, where they kicked off the second tour just as they had done the first. The guys spent the better part of the days practicing their new songs they'd be performing live for the first time, while Sophie and I read, played Candy Crush, and watched movies. The closer we got to Sin City, the thicker the anticipation and exhilaration grew in the air. Once we pulled up to the Hard Rock Hotel and Casino, we were caught in a whirlwind of excitement and deadlines. After Mason demanded that I be with him at all times, I followed him from interview to interview, and then to make-up and wardrobe for a photo shoot. I tried my best to blend into the wall wherever we went, never wanting to be an issue or distraction for him. We were given an hour break for him to freshen up and grab a bite to eat, but he spent over half of that time showing me how much he appreciated I was there with him. I didn't dare complain.

After their amazing show that night, I had one of the most eye-opening experiences of my life. I thought I knew what to expect—Sophie had warned me; not to mention I'd read plenty of rock star romances detailing what takes place at concert after-parties—but oh my word, nothing could've prepared me for what I witnessed. Thankfully, Mase kept me glued to his side the entire night, but even that didn't stop the skanks from throwing themselves at him, as if I simply didn't exist. And by throwing themselves, I mean rubbing their boobs against him, purposely flashing their panty-less crotches, attempting to sit on his lap, and a couple girls even walked up and kissed him on the mouth—all right in front of my face. Fucking shameless cunts.

He snubbed them all, openly rejecting their advances, and pulled me closer to him each time. His reaction to their brazen behavior reassured me that I was who he truly wanted to be with, and despite their saline-enhanced breasts and collagen-injected lips, I honestly wasn't concerned about him cheating on me. I accepted the fact he was a budding rock star, and unfortunately, these women were a part of the deal; if I couldn't trust him to be faithful, we had no chance whatsoever in making it work. I refused to live my life questioning his devotion and trustworthiness. Thoughts about how different he acted on the previous tour did cross my mind, but I never asked about it. Nothing good could've come from that conversation.

A little after two in the morning, he said he'd had enough and we retired to our hotel room, where I repaid him for his generosity earlier in the afternoon, and congratulated him for an incredible performance. The following afternoon, we departed the oasis in the desert after another round of sweet love-making, taking advantage of our last night alone for nearly two weeks, and began a string of nights similar to the one previous. Even though Jobu's Rum was doing well on the charts and selling out the venues weeks in advance, they were still relatively new on the scene and needed to hit up as many cities as possible on the tour, all while being fiscally responsible. For us, this meant leaving most places in the middle of the night, so after each show, we would hit up the post-performance festivities for a couple of hours and then all load up on the bus for Ed to lead us on our overnight trek.

In addition to the hordes of groupies in every city we stopped in, Andi's prediction of my fame did come true in a way. Within twenty-four hours of first being photographed with Mase in Vegas, my picture appeared on the website of nearly every tabloid and celebrity-tracking news services in the country. At first, the headlines were funny, as everyone wondered who the lead singer's leading lady was. Always smiling and gracious, I was polite to the paparazzi, even as I frequently dodged personal questions about myself, and mercifully, most of them seemed to like me. Mason made the mistake of calling me 'Angel' in front of them while in Denver, and I quickly became known as 'Cheerful Cherub'. Once the novelty of the two of us as a couple wore off—which occurred as soon as Hollywood's latest starlet was charged with possession of a narcotic—we were left alone for the most part.

The hardest part of adjusting to life on the bus was learning how to live with Cruz and Sebastian. Sure, Mase got on my nerves from time to time, but I loved him and could overlook his annoying habits; as for Sophie and Aaron, he was reserved and quiet, while she and I developed a great friendship and used each other as a sounding board when we were alone. However, Cruz and Sebastian—bless their hearts—were two single, young guys taking full-advantage of all the sexual perks their new fame offered; not to mention, they were messy as shit, leaving a trail of clutter behind them everywhere they went. Sophie and I unsuccessfully tried our best to train them to throw away trash, put their soiled clothes in a hamper, and to wash their dirty dishes, but like other aspects of the life that weren't so glamorous, I learned to deal with it.

Despite my complaints about the women, the lack of privacy, and the filthy roommates, I really enjoyed being on tour with Mason. Each time I watched him perform, I fell in love with him a little more. The music flowed freely from him like warmth from the sun, entrancing audiences who basked in his captivating rays. In addition, waking up snuggled in his arms every morning made me feel cherished and secure. I knew better than anyone no one was guaranteed another day, so I treasured all the time we spent together, and supported him completely as he chased his dream.

Footsteps approaching the living room once again pull me from my memories. Hastily, I put all of the photos on the floor back in with the others, and pretend to be overly-interested in a box of kitchen utensils.

"Have you made any progress?" Mason asks as he wipes the sweat from his brow.

Gazing up at him, I smile innocently and shrug my shoulders. "I'm trying, but it feels like these boxes keep multiplying." *There. That wasn't a lie.*

"Why don't we break for a bite to eat, and then we can focus on what we need for the night? Tomorrow, we can tackle the rest of this stuff together," he offers sincerely, "and then hopefully, we'll have a little time to ourselves on Monday before Crazy One and Crazy Two arrive."

Hopping to my feet, I tiptoe around the mess to where he stands and place a soft kiss on his salty lips. "Sounds good. What do you want me to get?" Silently, I pray he doesn't say McDonald's.

"McDonald's," he replies without hesitation. The boy is seriously going to turn into a French fry one day. "You know what I like."

"I think the entire world knows what you like. You're probably the only person that asks for fifty-piece order of chicken nuggets, two large fries, and seven sweet-n-sour dipping sauces to be in their dressing room before a concert, love.

He playfully swats my ass as I search for my purse and keys. "What can I say? I'm unique."

Before leaving the house on the food run, I glance over to the corner where the photos sit; I'm dying to continue going through them, but I know I need to focus on other things right now.

Chapter Four

Under Pressure

(Kiss You Inside Out ~ Hedley)

SCARLETT

After scarfing down yet another grease-soaked McDonald's meal, Mason and I work on setting up the master bedroom and en suite bathroom. We've been living in the two-bedroom apartment he's had since before we met, but now that he's finished touring and the twins are getting ready to start kindergarten in a few months, it's important for us to settle down in a neighborhood with exemplary schools—not to mention the need for a house large enough to properly host guests and to celebrate holidays.

Excited about our new home, I may have gone a little overboard in buying new sheets, comforters, throw pillows, rugs, and curtains for all four of the bedrooms, as well as new towels, soap dispensers, toothbrush holders, and other miscellaneous items for the bathrooms. The day I brought home the multiple oversized bags from Bed Bath & Beyond, I thought Mason was going to freak out, but thankfully, he didn't. Instead, he only made me promise he wouldn't be sleeping in pink satin sheets.

A little more than an hour later, our bed is dressed in fabrics of eucalyptus green and charcoal gray, and the bathroom is adorned with stainless steel accessories featuring frosted cerulean accents. Even though the rooms still need framed art and other decorative touches, everything looks incredible together. I'm trying hard not to laugh as Mason fights with the rod over the window, attempting to hang the light-blocking curtains, but when the metal clangs to the hardwood floor for the third time, I can't help myself. Bursting into a fit of giggles, I throw myself onto the freshly-made bed and hide my face in a pillow.

"You remember what happened last time you thought you were so funny, don't you?" he taunts from atop the ladder.

Unable to speak through my fit of hilarity, the creaking of the metal steps warns me he's coming, and for some reason, that makes me laugh even harder. Moments later, the mattress dips with his weight, and before I know it, his strong hands roll me over onto my back.

"You're getting our new comforter all dirty, woman," he drawls as he pushes the loose strands of hair out of my face.

Finally able to talk, I shake my head and reply, "No, I'm not. You're the grimy one who's been moving furniture all day."

"Oh, that's right. While I was busting my ass in the smoldering heat, you were inside the air-conditioned house pretending to work."

Popping up off my back, I climb in his lap and straddle his hips. "That's not true!" I exclaim. "I helped carry boxes inside this morning, and I *was* working inside the living room. I've been a good little wife today; I even went to get you McDonald's."

He smiles widely before leaning in to tenderly kiss my lips. "Mhmm, my good little *wife*," he mumbles against my mouth. "I like the way that sounds."

"Me too, my sexy *husband.*" Slipping my hands around his neck, I run my fingers over his buzzed hair and nip playfully at the ring he still wears in the right-side of his bottom lip at my request. It's fucking sexy. "Now why don't we forget about the drapery for tonight, and test out the water pressure in our new shower instead?"

Sliding off the bed with my limbs still wrapped snugly around him, he pads across the room towards the bathroom. "I'm gonna show you pressure, all right."

Within minutes of walking through the doorway, he silently strips us both naked and turns the hot water knob to full blast. Stepping under the vigorous spray of the showerhead, the water pelts my ivory skin, kneading the taut muscles and unraveling any tension left in my body. I feel him move in behind me; his sinewy frame presses against my back as he reaches around me to grab the shampoo. Waiting breathlessly for what's about to come, a small moan escapes my lips the moment his fingertips make contact with my scalp. Working it into a thick lather, he massages the rosemary-infused suds all through my hair. But he doesn't stop there.

His busy fingers continue to travel down my neck to my shoulders and back until he reaches my bottom. Then, leaving one hand on my ass, he glides the other across my hipbone to the front of my body, cupping in-between my legs and pulling my body flush against his. My soapy head rests back on his left shoulder with my eyes closed tightly, while his fingertip teases my lower lips, flicking back and forth over my swollen clit. After sensually rinsing the soap from my hair, he kisses and nibbles the slippery skin of my neck and shoulder as his finger brushes tantalizingly and slowly across my slit, yearning for the pressure he promised. The heated water falling down around our bodies adds another layer of lusty haze to the already-steamy atmosphere. Reaching down between our slick forms, I grab his fully-erect cock that's pressing into my ass and begin to stroke it fervently. I want him inside of me. Now.

"Slow down, Angel. We've got no reason to rush," he rasps into my ear. Grumbling, I gradually decrease the speed of my hand, making each pump deliberate and measured. "That's it, my good little wife," he commends, rewarding me with a dip of his finger into my core.

Unhurriedly moving his digit in and out of me, my legs weaken as the ache deep inside me builds. Suddenly, he removes his hand and spins me around to face him, a devilish grin playing on his face as he drops to his knees and looks up at me through his thick eyelashes, the droplets molding them into dark spikes. "I need to make sure all of the soap is rinsed off."

I brace myself with one hand up against the shower wall as he buries his face in my apex, devouring my yearning pussy with his lips and tongue. Lapping. Kissing. Sucking. Torturing me until I pass the point of no return. Palming his scalp—his hair too short to twist my fingers in—I hold his head tightly against my body and feed him my juices. My legs shake and threaten to give out on me, but thankfully, he quickly rises to his full-height and wraps his strong arm around my waist.

"Yep. All clean," he growls huskily. "Time to put you to bed."

Somehow, he manages to turn the shower off and get us both out and dried off. Stumbling to the bed, with our hands roaming each other's body, any notion of *slow* is thrown out the window. As soon as my back hits the mattress, he's plunging deep inside of my throbbing pussy. Placing my legs up on his shoulders to give him better leverage, he thrusts in and out feverishly, caressing the sensitive area of my core with the tip of his erection. The pressure inside of me builds faster than I can ever remember, my body enslaved to his touch, and within mere minutes, my walls clamp down around his shaft and I'm calling out his name, coating him in my sensual gratification. Moments later, he stiffens, and *that* look washes over his face just before he fills me with his warm seed.

Collapsing next to me on the bed, he loops his arms around my waist and cuddles me close. He kisses my forehead, each of my eyelids, the tip of my nose, and finally, my lips before whispering, "I love you, Angel. Sweet dreams."

"Goodnight, Mase. I love you too."

Chapter Five

City of Angels

(Angel ~ Jack Johnson)

SCARLETT

Waking up in the middle of the night in our new home, it takes me a few moments to grasp my bearings and remember where I am. The luster of the moonlight shines through the room at a different angle than our old place, and the deafening silence of no televisions or radios being on is a bit unnerving. Twisting at the waist, I peer over at Mase where he sleeps soundly, his chest rising and falling with each deep breath. We're both naked, and I realize we must've passed out immediately after having sex.

I lie there for a few minutes trying to fall back asleep, but to no avail. Slithering off the bed ninja-style trying not to wake him, I tiptoe over to the freshly-stocked dresser and grab some panties and a sleep-shirt. I quietly put them on and sneak out of the room to get a glass of water. However, en route to the kitchen I pass through the living room, and the container of photos in the corner calls out to me, begging me to go through a few more. My feet answer their plea, and before I know it, I'm sitting cross-legged in front of them and opening the lid.

Setting aside the ones I've already gone through, I pull out another batch, and tears of joy flood my eyes at first glance. The pictures are from the private concert the band played at Hotel Café in Los Angeles—the concert for me.

Life on the road with my rock-star boyfriend definitely had its ups and downs. After a couple of months, I thought I'd faced pretty much anything the lifestyle could throw at me. I realized the overzealous girls weren't going to go away, Cruz and Sebastian were going to continue to act like the sloppy, horny bachelors they were, and every outfit and hairstyle I wore would be equally loved and hated by the fashion critics. That was, until one of the tabloids somehow found out about Evie and Ash.

People are ruthless. Overnight, my nickname changed to "Angel of Death," and everywhere I went, I was questioned about why everyone close to me dies and how long it would be until I killed Mason. Not only did these stories and questions bring back terribly painful memories, but they grew into vicious lies about what an awful person I was. They portrayed me as a malicious, cold-hearted bitch that triggered both of their deaths, and some even suggested I murdered them.

Needless to say, I didn't handle any of it well; I refused to go out in public, spending nearly two weeks without getting off the bus. I withdrew myself from everyone, including Mason. When he tried to discuss things with me, I'd sit silently and cry, and when he'd attempt to hold or kiss me, I'd retract from his touch. It didn't take long for the media to notice my disappearance from shows and other outings, and the reports about our break-up followed shortly thereafter, claiming he dumped me in fear for his life.

One evening in Seattle, I was sitting alone in Cerrano, reading yet another depressing book while wallowing in my misery, when I heard a tap on the fiberglass door. Groaning, I rolled out of bed assuming I'd have to tell some other desperate groupie to get lost, so imagine my surprise when I swung the door open to see Heather's face as she stood in the parking lot.

"Oh my God, he wasn't lying—you do look like shit," she said as she snarled her nose up at me. "You've lost way too much weight."

"It's great to see you too," I quipped back. "Did you come all this way to give me a makeover and make me eat a cheeseburger?"

Pushing past me into the bus, she dropped her bag on the closest chair and put her hands on her hips. "No, I've come to pull your head out of your ass, and to remind you that these stupid fucks know nothing about you or what you've been through. We've talked about this—you were dealt a shitty hand and lost two people you loved dearly. Neither of them would want you to be playing this victim role; they'd want you to put up a fight and show these dumb asses that despite what they print, you are a young woman full of life, love, and laughter."

I collapsed on the couch and sighed dramatically. "What am I supposed to do, Heather?"

"You can start with taking a shower and getting dressed. I've been here less than five minutes and you're already depressing me," she snapped, sitting down next to me. "Don't you see you're letting them win? You've already had Evie and Ash ripped from your life—you had no choice in that—but you can *choose whether to allow them to take Mason and your current happiness, or to stand up and fight for him, yourself, and what you know is the truth. He loves you. He wants to be with you. He knows that you had nothing to do with what happened to them. Shouldn't he be all that matters? Not a bunch of strangers that truly know nothing?"*

I found it hard to argue with her logic, so I said nothing. Over the next few days, Heather stayed on the bus with us as we slowly traveled down the west coast. By the third day, I'm not sure if I was convinced all of her positive mumbo-jumbo talk was true, or if I was simply tired of listening to her, but I promised her if she went home I would get back out in the public eye, let Mason back in again—emotionally and physically—and ignore all of the haters in my life.

The morning we pulled into San Francisco, the guys left for a round of radio station interviews and photo shoots, so Heather took it upon herself to make me an appointment at a local hair salon. After I'd been shampooed, colored, cut, and styled, I really did feel like a new person. In actuality, it wasn't a huge change from my usual look, but considering I'd been rocking a bun for quite some time, the highlights and trim provided just enough newness to put a spring in my step. After the salon, we spent a few hours shopping, and I picked up several new outfits to wear to the upcoming California concerts. I wanted to look my best for Mason, knowing that the next week was a big deal for the band as they performed their way down the California coast, especially the show at the Staples Center in Los Angeles the following Thursday.

That night, Heather flew back to Houston, claiming that her job was done, and I surprised Mase by showing up at the concert presenting my freshly-styled locks and a sexy new dress. I'll never forget seeing his eyes light up when he caught a glimpse of me enjoying his voice in the right wing of the stage. As soon as they finished the show, he hurried over to me and picked me up in his strong arms, twirling me around while kissing all over my face. We didn't make it to the after-party that night; we had lost time to make up for.

Almost instantly, Mase and I found our groove as a couple again, and by the time we crossed into Orange County, it was as if nothing had ever happened. During the first couple of days, pictures of the two of us back together out in public made a few headlines, but I avoided the media like the plague and focused on what I knew to be the truth.

Everyone on the tour was overly-excited about the LA show. Not only did performing in the entertainment capital of the world incite an electrifying buzz, but we were staying there four days for two shows, which meant three nights in a hotel, and a day-and-a-half of free time! I couldn't wait to soak in a bathtub, and to sprawl out naked across a big bed without worrying about other people sleeping a few feet from Mase's and my bed.

The first night, they played at the Staples Center, and everything about it was insane. The intensity of the crowd overpowered the massive venue, the band unveiled their new single—which the concert-goers responded wildly to, and the after-party was full of familiar faces from the big screen. I tried hard not to be star-struck, but it was nearly impossible, and to think these celebrities had come out to see my boyfriend sing was just mind-blowing.

The following evening, the band was scheduled to perform an intimate show at the famous Hotel Café. Everyone on the guest list were fans who had won tickets for this private performance on a local radio station over the previous month. During the day, the guys were busy with interviews and photo shoots with the station, and even though I had just been to the salon with Heather a week prior, Sophie and I hit up a day spa, where we indulged ourselves in massages, facials, manicures, and pedicures, all while sipping pink champagne. We talked about everything and nothing, laughing and relaxing as we thoroughly enjoyed our girl-time together.

On the way back to the hotel, Mason texted me that the band landed a dinner meeting with a producer they'd wanted to work with, and that Sophie and I were to meet them at the performance that night at nine. Our names would be on the list. I didn't think much about it, quickly replying with a "Kk. See you then."

Deciding to extend our girl-date, she and I arranged to change into our evening attire, and then meet back downstairs for dinner and drinks before the show. For the big show the previous day, I'd dressed up in a sexy black number with matching heels, my hair in a fancy up-do, and my make-up more dramatic than normal. It was fun to get all dolled-up and hang out with all the pretty people, but my feet were still killing me, so I elected to go with a more casual, relaxed look that night. After slipping my slender legs into a pair of fitted indigo jeans, I opted for a sheer, silvery blouse adorned with fine, metallic strands threaded sporadically throughout it, my snowy-white satin push-up bra clearly visible under the delicate fabric. I allowed my subtly-highlighted tresses to cascade into soft waves down my back, while opting for light make-up application—a thin coat of mascara to lengthen my already dark lashes, a touch of cerise blush to highlight the freckles sprinkled across my cheekbones, and a hint of coconut-flavored gloss smeared across my lips. Before sliding my feet into strappy, silver sandals and grabbing the matching handbag off the bed, I did a once-over in the hotel bathroom mirror, pleased with my appearance—flirty and fun.

I glanced at the alarm clock on the night stand, realizing I was five minutes late, so I hurriedly stuffed my license, money, room key, and phone into the clutch and rushed out into the hallway, the door slamming shut behind me. A quick elevator ride down to the lobby, and I found Sophie at the bar enjoying a pre-dinner glass of wine. Sliding up next to her, she greeted me with a huge smile and a hug, as if we hadn't seen each other in years.

"You look absolutely perfect, Scarlett. I can't wait for tonight," she exclaimed. I thought her excitement level was unusually elevated, but chalked it up to our day of bonding and knowing that the guys had the following day completely free of appointments or shows. I knew she missed hanging out with Aaron, and had a day of activities planned for them.

"Thank you. So do you," I replied sincerely. I was pleased to see she was dressed similarly in a silky red top, tight faded jeans, and black ballet flats. "Where do you want to eat?"

"I made us reservations at Beso. It's pretty close to the Hotel Café, so we can just walk over there when we're finished." She swallowed the last of her wine, and grabbed her purse from the bar-top as she hopped off the seat.

Shadowing her, we headed out the main doors and made our way to the restaurant. Dinner was excellent; we shared several different items for a sampler effect, and the drinks were even better. I lost count of how many Pretty Girls—their signature drink—I consumed; it was flowing like ice-cold lemonade on a hot summer day. Before I knew it, she announced it was time to go, so we finished up our last drink and paid the tab before heading out.

Exiting into the warm summer evening, I paused for a moment just outside the door, and I closed my eyes while deeply inhaling the southern California air. Tipsy, but not drunk, the alcohol in my blood tingled under my skin. I felt alive and energetic, optimistic and confident. Sophie grabbed my hand and began dragging me down the pavement, insisting we couldn't be late for some reason or another. I giggled and followed her lead, high on a lot of life and a little Grey Goose, excited to hear the show, and to spend the next day alone with my Mase.

We entered the coffee-shop-turned-music-venue, and were quickly ushered to a reserved table right up next to the small stage. Taking a look around the narrow space, the brick-walled room elicited a cozy, inviting ambiance with its dim lighting and high ceilings. A server hurried over to us the moment we were seated, welcoming us by name and getting our drink order, and the murmuring buzz filling the air in the packed room was nearly tangible as everyone waited for Jobu's Rum to take the stage. Completely enthralled by the ambiance of the quaint music café, my body began to hum with exhilaration, eager to see Mason sing this up-close and personal.

Shortly after our first drinks arrived, the crowd burst into applause and cheers as the guys casually strolled onto the stage. They all look relaxed and fully at ease in the informal setting, even though it was completely different than what they had grown accustomed to. Mason was dressed in his typical solid black t-shirt that showed off his tatted sleeves, loose jeans, and black Chucks; his hair was recently buzzed, and his lip-ring glimmered every time the light hit it just right. Looking down at where I sat, his lips curled into a playful grin and his eyes twinkled with secretive mischief as he grabbed the microphone and began talking.

"Good evening, Hollywood! It's great to see y'all here tonight." It'd been noted time and time again he had a way of talking to his audience that made people feel like he was having a personal chat with them. Fans couldn't help but love him. "We truly appreciate you all coming out to witness this once-in-a-lifetime kind of show. I know you were all promised an 'intimate performance', but you have no idea how intimate we're going to get tonight."

Confused, I tore my eyes away from his lean figure and looked over at Sophie, who was busy blowing kisses and making googley-eyes at Aaron. She was paying no mind to me whatsoever, and I couldn't get her attention without calling to her out loud, so instead, I refocused on Mason.

"We're gonna start off by playing a few of our favorites from the first album, and then our two new singles from the second," he continued. "After that, we've got a little something special for you."

Immediately, they began their set, nailing each song flawlessly, playing with a zealous passion that pulsated deep inside me. It had been so long since I'd watched from the audience as he performed—typically, I watched from the wings of the stage—and it was a truly different experience looking into his eyes as he crooned the lyrics. As the song they had just debuted the night before came to an end, Mason grabbed a wooden stool sitting on the side of the stage and dragged it over to where he stood. The music stopped, and everyone—myself included—remained silent, watching and waiting with ardent curiosity.

Palming the neck of the microphone, he affectionately gazed down at me and smiled warmly, extending his hand down in my direction. "Scarlett, will you join me up here, please?"

Surprised. Startled. Dumbfounded. A thousand other emotions I couldn't pinpoint roared to life inside of me.

Scattered cheers and whistles echoed throughout the otherwise soundless room as I unquestioningly stood up and joined him, nervous my shaky legs were going to collapse underneath me.

"Sit down," he instructed, pointing at the stool.

Doing as he requested, I hopped up on the circular, wooden surface as he traded his electric guitar for an acoustic one waiting for him off to the side. I didn't need to look at my reflection in a mirror to know my cheeks were severely blush-stained and my green eyes were enlarged to the size of saucers, unsure of what was happening.

The stares of the audience fixed on me. My gaze fixed on him.

Without another word, his fingers strummed the guitar and the opening chords of "Your Guardian Angel" resonated loudly throughout the room. My face lit up, remembering the first time I'd heard him sing that song—the morning after I'd come back from being gone after Evie's death. He'd been cooking breakfast for me and was unaware I was watching him; I'd snuck up behind him and whispered in his ear, "I'll stay with you, Mase."

After he sang the first verse and chorus, he somehow morphed the song into Robbie Williams' "Angel" without missing a beat, and then a little bit later, he did it again with the Aerosmith song of the same name. Magically, he'd comprised a compilation of songs about angels, perfectly interweaving the lyrics and transitioning the harmonies so that it flowed faultlessly. Tears of unadulterated joy spilled down my cheeks, and I didn't bother to wipe them away. The final part of the angel anthology was Jack Johnson's rendering of the namesake, and as he sang the powerful, awe-inspiring lyrics...I knew.

I simply knew.

And the answer was yes.

The song came to an end, and he propped the guitar up against one of the nearby amps. Then, in his sensual baritone voice—his grey eyes glimmering—he spoke directly to my heart. "Hollywood is known as the land of dreams. Los Angeles is the City of Angels." Pausing to lick his dry lips, I found his nervousness endearing and sexy. "So I figured, what better place to make my dreams come true and ask my angel to be my wife?" He dropped to both knees in front of me as he pulled a ring out of his pocket. The world around us metamorphosed into obscurity; nothing else mattered in that moment. With hands slightly shaking, he slid the solitaire onto my left ring finger. "Scarlett Alexandria MacGregor, will you marry me?"

I'm not sure I ever actually said yes; instead, I sprung from the stool into his arms, tackling him to the floor. My mouth crashed down on his boldly and unapologetically, answering him first with my lips and then my tongue in what had to be the most ungraceful kiss ever.

Ask me if I cared. I was going to be Mrs. Scarlett Templeton.

Over five years later and I still remember that night as if it was yesterday—hands down, one of the top-three moments of my life. Browsing through the photos of the two of us up on the stage, the euphoric glow on our faces is undeniable. We had no idea in that moment of the curve balls that would be thrown our way shortly after, but for that night, my life felt like a fairy tale.

Chapter Six

Two Lines, Two Beats

(This ~ Ed Sheeran)

SCARLETT

Looking around for a clock in my new living room, all I can see are the towers of boxes surrounding me on the floor. I need to get up and get some water anyhow—it was the real reason I got out of bed to begin with—so I rise to my feet and quietly scamper into the kitchen. The clock on the stove reads three-fifteen as I grab a cold bottle from the fridge. My sensible self is telling me I really need to go back to sleep, otherwise I'm going to be dragging ass tomorrow when I need to be productive, but I shush her with a promise I'll only stay up another thirty minutes.

Kneeling down next to the photos scattered on the floor, I excitedly submerge my arm into the storage container and draw out another small pile. Immediately, my eyes are drawn to several in the stack that are larger than the rest, and are printed on a different type of material. Staring down at the black and white sonogram pictures, I beam internally. I think back to the day we found out our lives would change forever.

After Mason proposed in LA, our relationship only continued to grow and strengthen. I knew we couldn't even think about getting married until after the tour ended, and even then, I'd have to find out what their schedule would be for the next tour. I didn't mind though; I was confident it would happen someday. The display of love and adoration he showed me—not only during the proposal, but each and every day—spoke volumes about what I meant to him. In the rare times I did feel insecure or lacked confidence, all I had to do was look at my charm bracelet circling my right wrist and the diamond solitaire sitting atop my ring finger and I was reminded of his loyalty and faithfulness.

As the tour progressed, Jobu's Rum steadily climbed the charts and increased in popularity as they played more shows. When the third single on their second album hit the top-five overall, we were in Oklahoma City, close to the halfway mark of the tour. That night after the show, we all went out to celebrate their amazing accomplishment, but after about an hour of being at the bar, I began to feel sick. A sudden onset of nausea, chills, and overall body aches hit me out of nowhere.

Insisting that Mason stayed out with his friends, I somehow made it back to the bus, and instantly passed out cold on my bed. I didn't remember them coming back, but the next morning, he told me I still had my shoes on and my coin purse clutched in my hand when he found me. Unfortunately, the light of a new day didn't bring any reprieve from the awful feelings, nor did the next. Finally, after four days straight with no improvement, Sophie asked Ed to take us to a pharmacy so she could purchase some different medicines. The guys were at a sound check when she entered the area that was my "room" and tossed a plastic Walgreen's bag down on the comforter next to my lethargic body.

"I think you need that," she said matter-of-factly, standing in the doorway waiting for me to do something.

Groaning, I bent over at the waist to retrieve the bag, expecting to pull out some kind of drugs, but instead, I pulled out a pregnancy test. My questioning eyes flashed up to hers, asking the words I couldn't muster the strength to speak.

"How long's it been since you had your period, Scarlett?" Sitting down on the bed next to me, her voice took on a comforting tone as she soothingly rubbed my unshaven calf.

"I don't know," I croaked. "I have a hard time keeping up with time on this bus."

"Take the test, please. If it comes back negative, we need to get you to a doctor to find out what's wrong. If this was a stomach bug, at least one other of us would've gotten it, being that we live in such close quarters."

Her words rang with truth, but I'd felt so terrible; I hadn't even thought about the possibility of pregnancy. "Okay, I'll take it. Can you help me get up?" I hated feeling so puny and whiney, but because I hadn't eaten in so long, my strength was completely diminished.

"Of course," she replied with an encouraging smile.

Taking hold of my hands, she slid me to the end of the bed and helped me the few feet to the bathroom she and I shared. She opened the box and handed me the stick. "Just pee on this part and put the lid back on. Then we wait three minutes for the results—two lines means positive; one line is negative," she instructed.

I nodded and closed the sliding pocket door, unsure if I was shivering with nerves, illness, or a little bit of both. I managed to pee a little bit—my body was so dehydrated from the lack of fluids I'd been able to keep down—and I hoped it was enough for an accurate reading. Doing as I was told, I covered the stick with the lid and sat it down on the side of the sink to wash my hands.

I didn't even get the soap pumped into my hands before two blue lines glared up at me from the results window. The breath escaped my lungs in one whoosh as the little bit of color I still had in my face drained rapidly. If I hadn't been frozen into a statuesque form of myself, I'm sure I would've panicked...screamed...vomited...something. But I stood there unmoving, staring at the plastic object that mocked me and all of the plans I had for my future.

"Are you okay?" Sophie called out. "Are you getting sick again?"

Silence.

"Scarlett? Answer me! What's going on?"

More silence.

She must've figured it out after a few minutes, because the next thing I recall was her looping her arms around my waist, hugging me and telling me everything was going to be okay.

But she was wrong. Nothing was going to be okay.

Sophie stayed with me that night instead of going to the show; neither of us said much. I knew I had to tell Mason soon, but I didn't know how. My emotions followed the second-hand of the clock, whirling through my mind in a circular motion. Worry. Fear. Anxiety. Hope. Apprehension. Helplessness. Excitement. Worry. Fear.

Over and over, I couldn't escape it.

I finally passed out from exhaustion at some point, only waking up when Mason slipped into bed next to me. I curled into his warm body and clung to him, wanting to blurt it out, but knowing it wasn't the time.

"Hey there, Angel," he whispered, pulling me close. "You feeling any better?"

"A little, I guess. I'm just really tired."

Kissing me on the forehead, he nodded. "Get some sleep. Hopefully, you'll feel better in the morning."

Morning came, and of course, I didn't feel any better. I spent the better part of an hour dry-heaving into the white porcelain bowl of death, trying to be as quiet as possible since I knew everyone else was still asleep. Sophie was waiting for me with a glass of ginger ale and graham crackers when I emerged, and she sat with me at the table as I sipped and nibbled, hoping it would stay down.

"There you two are," Mason greeted us cheerfully as he slid into the chair next to me wearing nothing but a pair of pajama pants hung low on his hips. Kissing me on the cheek, he gave me a once-over and shook his head. "We're going to take you to an urgent care clinic as soon as we get into Kansas City."

I shook my head and waved my hand in front of my face. "That's not necessary. I'll get better, eventually."

"It's non-negotiable, Scarlett," he replied in a stern voice I wasn't used to hearing from him. As if he immediately felt bad, he wrapped his arm around my shoulders and pulled me into him. "Well, I do have a little bit of good news you missed out on last night. Maybe this will cheer you up some."

"Oh, really? What happened?" Sophie asked curiously.

A proud smile covered his face. "The producer we met with in LA wants us to record our next album with him as soon as this tour finishes up, and Owen locked in the dates for our third tour, which will include some international venues. I hope you girls like life on the road 'cause it doesn't look like we're going home anytime soon."

Instantaneously, I burst into uncontrollable tears at his announcement, confusing the hell out of him, and prompting a look of empathy from her.

"What's wrong? Did I say something wrong?" His head swiveled back and forth between me and Sophie.

"I'm pregnant, Mase," I blurted out in-between my blubbering sobs. It wasn't how I planned to tell him. Shit, I still hadn't even figured that part out either, but it definitely wasn't going to be in front of another person while stuck on the bus traveling down the highway.

At first, I didn't look up at him, petrified to see the look of disappointment or abhorrence playing on his face. Sophie excused herself to leave us alone to discuss things, even though I secretly wished she'd stay—she was my security blanket.

"Let's go to our room and talk about it," he said in a hushed voice.

I nodded and stood up, and then he did something that shocked me. He scooped me up in his arms, kissed my lips tenderly, and carried me to the back of the bus, where he gently laid me on top of the bed. Lying down next to me, he wrapped me in his arms and held my face snugly up against his bare chest as he lightly stroked my hair. We stayed like that for a few minutes, both trying to find the words that matched our thoughts.

Eventually, he pulled back from me a bit so we could look into each other's eyes before he began to talk. "Angel, I can only imagine what you're thinking and feeling right now—God knows my head is all over the place—but the one thing I'm not wavering on at all is that this baby is a blessing. I know we haven't talked about it, but I assumed one day in the future we were going to have a family. We're already engaged, we love each other unconditionally, and we're just speeding up the family thing a bit."

Unsure of how to even respond, I started to cry again.

"It's okay; it's okay. We're gonna figure this out together," he reassured me. "Our entire relationship hasn't followed the traditional path of doing things, so there's no reason to start now."

That prompted a small chuckle from me, and I wiped the wetness from my cheeks with the back of my hand. "Mason, I don't think you're realizing what this means. I won't be able to tour with you anymore once I have the baby. We'll be apart all the time. Plus, I don't know the first thing about how to take care of a baby!"

His hands moved up to my face, cupping under my chin as his thumbs brushed softly across my tear-stained jaw. "Listen to me, Scarlett. We will figure this out; we are NOT going to be apart. You've always told me you believe strongly in fate—everything happens for a reason, right?"

"Right," I murmured, still unsure I believed what he was saying.

"It's all about perspective, Angel. I'm choosing to view this baby as a blessing, a creation made from our love."

With those words, he leaned in and kissed me. Carefully. Cautiously. He softly grazed his lips against mine several times before his tongue slowly swept over my bottom lip. Moaning instinctively, my mouth parted slightly, inviting him in for a more sensual kiss. His hands slid from my jaw, down to my neck, and finally into my hair, his fingers twisting into the locks hanging loose at my nape. Our tongues met halfway, lazily rolling and winding around each other, dancing to the tune of our hearts beating. So many words were spoken in that kiss without a single sound.

Shortly after our talk, we both fell back asleep for a little while, only to be woken up by my need to throw up yet again. It was Mason that time waiting for me with the drink and crackers, which despite how awful I felt, made me smile. By then, everyone else was up and moving about the bus, so we decided to have a meeting to announce the baby news. We all agreed not to tell anyone else until I could get to a doctor and find out how far along I was. Also discussed was the band's exciting announcement from the previous night. Mason made it clear that our having a baby wouldn't impact them moving forward with their plans, and he instructed Owen to begin making whatever arrangements necessary to assure the baby and I would be travelling wherever they went.

Finding a doctor was another problem we had to address. We still had four months left of the tour, and with being in a different city every night, it wasn't like I could see the same one more than once. Owen got me an appointment for the following day in Kansas City, but we agreed I would need to find one in Houston I could travel to see every so often. Less than twenty-four hours after finding out Mason and I were going to be parents, some of the shock and fear began to leave my system, and it was replaced with a tiny morsel of excitement.

At the first doctor's visit, I could've sworn we were on an episode of Punk'd. It started with just Mason and me going to the appointment, knowing it'd be the only time we saw this doctor; we just wanted to confirm the pregnancy and get an idea of my progress. However, by the time we left the bus in the parking lot of the medical offices, the entire group was tagging along behind us, everyone excited about the 'band's baby'. I wish I could've recorded the facial expressions on the people in the waiting room and the office staff when the seven of us—four tattooed rockers, Sophie, Owen, and myself—strolled off of the elevator and into the obstetrician's office. Soon after checking in, I was ushered to the back for a urine specimen and blood work; I'm pretty sure they wanted to get us out of there as soon as humanly possible. I didn't wait long in the room for the nurse to come in and take my vitals, as well as ask me five hundred questions about my sexual history and past alcohol and drug use. I guessed I passed that part of the exam, because moments later, the doctor entered and greeted me with a bright smile.

"Hi there, you must be Scarlett," she said as she offered her hand to me, which I shook politely. "I'm Dr. Scott. It's a pleasure to meet you."

I wasn't sure what it was about her, but I liked her immediately. "It's nice to meet you too," I replied.

"So my nurse told me a little bit about your situation, but let me make sure I've got this straight. You're currently on tour with your fiancé's band, so you're just passing through here, and you recently took a home pregnancy test that came back positive. You don't know when you're last menstrual cycle was, and you've been experiencing fatigue and nausea for about a week." She looked up at me from the chart she held in her hand, awaiting my confirmation.

"That about sums it up," I murmured with a meek smile.

"Perfect. Well, from the urine sample you provided when you first got here, I can assure that you are pregnant, but without knowing your last cycle dates, the only way we'll be able to determine how far along you are is with an ultrasound. Is that okay with you?"

I nodded, allowing that sliver of excitement to grow a little bit more at the thought of seeing the baby on an ultrasound.

"Assuming you have a normal pregnancy, you'll be able to stay out on the road up until you're about seven months pregnant, and then I'd plan on spending the last eight-to-ten weeks at home, or wherever you're planning on having the baby. You'll need to go ahead and establish a relationship with a primary OB that you plan to have deliver the baby, and when

you do, just let my office know so we can send them all of the results from today's exam and labs to them. Okay?"

"I can do that. No problem."

"Great, now worst thing's first—I need to do a pelvic exam just to make sure everything looks okay, and then we can call in whomever you'd like from the waiting room so they can watch the ultrasound with you."

Thankfully, she sped through the exam portion of the appointment inflicting minimal discomfort, and then she left briefly to go get Mason. Minutes later, he entered the room with a huge smile, and I instantly felt calmer just being in his presence. He walked over to me where I lay on the exam table and gave me a quick kiss.

"You ready to see our little peanut, Mase?" I whispered.

Nodding, he grabbed my hand and squeezed it tightly to his chest. "You have no idea."

Dr. Scott reentered the room and got everything set up so we could all see the screen. She explained she was going to do the ultrasound inter-vaginally since I didn't have a full bladder, and told us to ask questions at any time. Within seconds, our eyes were glued to the monitor in front of us, waiting for her to explain what the amoeba-like structures floating around were. I noticed a look of surprise briefly flash across her face, followed by her jotting some notes down.

"I'm not quite sure how to say this, so I'm just going to be blunt." Glancing at me, Mason, and then back at the screen, she continued, "You see this? This is your baby's heart beating." She pointed at the screen, and the heartbeat inside of a little sea monkey looking thing was clearly evident. My own heart soared from seeing our little baby for the first time, and I peered over at Mason's face to see tears threatening to spill from his eyes; he smiled down at me and squeezed my hand even more tightly.

She moved the wand over a bit to focus on another similar pulsating form. "And this is your other *baby's heart beating. Congratulations—you're having twins!"*

Chapter Seven

Making a Splash

(Team ~ Lorde)

SCARLETT

Laughing out loud as I relive that day in my head, I still keep in touch with Dr. Scott even now. After the shock wore off enough that I could stand up and walk out of the examination room, she made me promise to let her know how the pregnancy progressed. She even asked Mason and the rest of the band for an autograph before we left. Whenever I had a question about anything at all, no matter how small, I knew I could always call or email her, and she'd advise me what to do, or let me know if it was normal or not. I only wish she could've been there when the twins were born. That was a delivery like no other.

Swinging my legs around underneath me so I'm kneeling over the container of photos, I dig through the ones remaining, trying to find some from their birthday. It doesn't take me long to locate them—all I had to look for was blue hair.

News of the twins spread like wildfire through the media. I refused to peruse celebrity news any longer—not wanting to see the headlines of how I trapped Mason into the engagement, or how I was going to birth two antichrists—so I didn't know what truth, if any, was being published. Everywhere we went, people would ask how I felt, how far along I was, if we had picked out names, etcetera. The questions were repetitive and got tiring, but I was always polite and courteous to the people who paid me the same respect.

We'd found out I was fourteen weeks the day of our appointment with Dr. Scott, which gave me a due date of roughly March third, give or take a week. The tour was set to end the last week of January, and the guys were supposed to record in LA beginning in February, so we chose a primary doctor there instead of Houston. Sophie and I flew out to meet her around my twenty-week mark, and even though she wasn't Dr. Scott-friendly, she was nice enough, and was understanding of my situation. Because I was carrying twins, and the likelihood I'd make it to full-term was slim, she requested I stop traveling at thirty weeks. I actually stayed on the bus until thirty-two weeks, because I was feeling great and desperately wanted to spend Christmas and New Year's with Mason and the gang.

Immediately after the first of the year, I moved into a hotel in the heart of LA by myself, while Jobu's Rum finished up the last three weeks of performances. At first, it was a bit overwhelming being big, pregnant, and all alone in a strange city, but I adjusted quickly. Mason and I FaceTimed with one another every morning when he woke up, and every night when he got ready for bed. I'd usually cry for a good five minutes each time we hung up, but I chalked it up to the raging hormones consuming my body. It wasn't out of the ordinary for Campbell's Soup commercials to ignite an onslaught of waterworks during that time. I spent the rest of my time reading and writing reviews for the blog I'd started in Evie's memory, going to my weekly doctor's visits, and walking the trails at a nearby park to stay somewhat active.

Before I knew it, the tour was over, and Mason and the band were all in LA with me. I was on cloud nine. Sophie threw me a surprise baby shower that Max, Andi, Mina, and Noah all flew out for. In addition, Ash's sister and mom attended, which meant so much to me; I couldn't express to them how elated I was that they came. In light of everyone being there together, Mason and I revealed the names of the babies at the party: Everett Matthew and Ashlynn Marley. As soon as everyone heard the names—knowing they were in honor of Evie and Ash—there wasn't a dry eye in the room. Two beautiful lives had been taken from us, but we were now being blessed with two new ones. I could only hope they were watching over us from above.

A week or so later, as we inched closer and closer to the due date, I found out about a huge author signing taking place that weekend in Hollywood. Jobu's Rum was scheduled to play at an outdoor festival in San Diego the same afternoon, and because it was so close, they weren't even going to stay the night; they'd just go down there for the show and head back. I knew the doctor had warned me about being on my feet for long periods of time, but I was feeling great, and with only four weeks to go 'til D-day, it appeared that I just might make it. I managed to get last minute tickets thanks to Kayla, a fellow blogger, and an amazing friend I'd made in the book world the previous year—and I talked Sophie into going with me. Unfortunately, the night before the event, her grandmother fell extremely ill and Sophie caught the first red-eye back to Houston.

Concerned about leaving me alone, Mason said he could cancel their appearance, but I insisted that he went. He'd only be gone about eight hours total with travel, and I would surely be okay in that timeframe. Secretly, I wanted him to go so I could still attend the signing, knowing damn well he would frown upon me going alone. I had dilated to a three, and was forty percent effaced at my previous doctor's appointment. She'd recommended I stay off my feet as much as possible, but I disregarded her suggestion, claiming I felt fine. Thankfully, he headed out in the late morning for the show, kissing me goodbye a thousand times and promising he'd be back as soon as possible.

Throughout the entire pregnancy, he was overly-attentive and thoughtful, doting on me every chance he got. His hands were always on my belly, especially once he could feel them kick. We would lie on the bed in the back of the bus for hours, and he would kiss my body from head to toe, telling me how beautiful I was and what a perfect mother I was going to be. Mercifully, the pregnancy didn't freak him out in regards to sex, because there were a couple months during the second trimester I felt like a sixteen-year-old boy. I couldn't get enough. All I wanted was to read erotica, and then I'd try to replicate whatever scene I'd envisioned in my head. He did draw the line at using restraints though, but promised me if I was still interested after the babies were born and when we were in our own place he'd take me up on the offer. I was counting the days.

As soon as he was gone, I hurriedly took a shower and began to get ready. I wanted to dress cute since I knew I'd be taking photos with some of my favorite authors, but seriously, how cute can a girl in her thirty-sixth week of pregnancy with twins really be? Every article of clothing I owned had an elastic waistband and a tie under the boobs. I threw on my one pair of designer maternity jeans and a flowy, black blouse, before blow-drying my long hair straight and putting on a touch of make-up. One great thing about being pregnant was with all the prenatal vitamins I'd been taking, my hair looked better than it ever had before. Not that my great hair was going to help alleviate the stretch marks across my lower abdomen and gigantic jugs that were once my cute, perky boobs. I wasn't sure how much these babies were planning on eating, but based strictly on my bra size, I was sure I could feed them for a good three years.

Once I was somewhat pleased with my reflection in the mirror, I slid my swollen feet in some flip flops, snagged my purse from the kitchen counter, and headed out the door. The cab ride was a short fifteen minutes, and as I walked up to the hotel where the event was being held, I started to get eager and anxious. Upon entering the room, I was handed a tote bag and a map of where the authors were sitting. In order to make it easy for everyone, they'd been set up in alphabetical order by their last name.

Gazing around the crowded room, I decided to start from the beginning to make sure I didn't miss anyone. The first table I stopped at was Belle Aurora's. Her novel, RAW, was one that I praised for weeks after reading it. It was so different than anything I'd read, and I truly fell in love with it from the very first page. From there, I stopped to purchase books from nearly every author in attendance. I couldn't restrain myself. Looking at the faces of the other readers there, I loved seeing the same glowing expression I was sure I sported. It was almost surreal to be in a room with this many authors I absolutely adored. When I reached Lisa De Jong's table, I spent a little longer there than at the others, as I told her about how I first started my blog, Ever Afters for Evie, with my review of "When It Rains". She was amazing to talk to, exuding so much appreciation and kindness she made me tear up—damn hormones.

Midway through, I had to take a break for water and to get another tote bag, since I had filled my first. The Braxton Hicks contractions started up as they always did when I was on my feet for a while, but I'd learned to power through. Several women asked me if I was okay, and I quickly assured them I was just taking a breather. After I downed the bottle of water, I set back out on my journey through row after row of authors, buying books and taking pictures the whole way. The cramping really started bothering me as I got to the back wall, but I was determined, knowing I probably wouldn't have this chance again for a really long time.

With three authors to go—three of my absolute faves—I pushed the nagging pain to the back of my mind and stepped up to Madeline Sheehan's table. I'd become a fan of hers first with the Holy Trinity Trilogy, but when I read Undeniable, I absolutely fell in love with Deuce. She made feeling dirty feel so good.

"I'll take Undeniable and Unbeautifully," I said with an unexpected grimace. I wanted to say so much more to her, like her uncanny ability to make me fall for people I shouldn't, and how I had sex on a motorcycle and thought about Deuce afterwards—okay, maybe that would've been a little weird—but the steadily increasing cramps stole my breath and my voice.

Her assistant handed her the two books as she peered up at me and smiled. "Who would you like these made out to?" she asked in a voice much softer than I expected.

"Scarlett, please," I choked out in-between breaths. I leaned forward to offer her the yellow sticky note attached to my finger with the correct spelling of my name, when suddenly, a surge of liquid gushed down my legs. Mortification—served warm and wet. Dropping the bags of books and grasping onto the table, it took my brain a few seconds to compute what was happening. Fuck me.

"Are you okay? Do you need to sit down?" The concern in Madeline's voice was evident.

Shaking my head slightly, I continued to use the table as a crutch, unsure of what to do next. "My water just broke," I slurred, biting the inside of my cheek as a sharp contraction shot through me.

"Oh fuck! Are you serious? Someone get some help," she called out to anyone and everyone in the vicinity.

A ruckus around me ensued as a bunch of strangers helped me shuffle over to a chair at a nearby table. Trying desperately to focus on what I needed to do, there were people in my face spouting question after question at me.

"Are you with anyone?" "Who should we call?" "Did you drive here?" "Should I call an ambulance?"

Inhaling and exhaling several deep breaths, I somewhat regained my composure as I looked down at the table where I was sitting. Copies of Ashley Suzanne's Mirage and Awakening were staring up at me, and when I glanced to my left and saw her sitting directly next to me, she grinned and said, "Now that's some kind of entrance, Mama." I laughed—well, I tried to, but I think it came out more like a growl.

When the pain subsided for a minute, I answered all of the questions as quickly as I could before the next contraction came. "I'm here alone. There's no one in town to call. I didn't drive; I came in a taxi. And yes, please call an ambulance, unless one of you knows how to deliver babies."

A streak of blue hair appeared from out of nowhere and knelt down in front of me. I looked down inquisitively, and Tara Sivec's cheerful face greeted me. "Hey there, sweets. The ambulance will be here in just a few minutes, okay? You don't have anyone you want me to call?"

"I need to text my fiancé; he's in San Diego, so it'll take him a while to get here. I don't have any other family local."

"You want me to come with you to the hospital? I'm an awesome cheerleader." Her offer was kind, but I wasn't going to ask her to accompany a stranger to the hospital. Following her on Facebook and Twitter, it felt as if I knew her like a close friend, but in reality, I was just another fan. I'd be fine alone.

"I'm okay. You don't have to do that, but thank—"

I didn't get the chance to complete my sentence, as the EMT's pushed through the crowd with a gurney, helped me up onto it, and then loaded me into the back of the ambulance. I swear the driver took the longest possible route to the hospital, stopped at lights that weren't even red, and aimed for every bump and pothole in the road. The technician in the back with me kept trying to ask questions about the pregnancy as he took my vitals and hooked me up to the oxygen machine, but the pain shooting through my body was rapidly becoming unbearable.

From my hours of reading online about the entire birthing process, I knew that my water breaking was only the beginning of active labor, and because it was my first pregnancy, it would most likely be a while until the twins were born. I don't think my babies received that message, because it felt as if they were trying to escape my body through any means necessary; I honestly thought my stomach was going to explode at any moment.

After what seemed like hours in that damn sterile box of a vehicle, I felt us come to a stop, and then the back doors opened, allowing the bright California sun to flood the space. Hurriedly, they got me out of the ambulance and wheeled me into the hospital through the emergency room, passing me off to a nurse waiting with a wheelchair. It was then that I realized I didn't have my purse with me; I had left it at the signing.

"I need someone to call my fiancé," I whined as we entered the elevator. "I don't have my purse or my phone."

"No worries, Ms. MacGregor, your sister has your personal belongings and is waiting for you in the room," the older female said calmly. "I believe she's already contacted him."

MY SISTER?!? Another contraction rocketed through my body, causing me to double over in agony before I had a chance to ask who my sister was. The elevator doors opened shortly after, and we continued the journey to the birthing suites I had toured only a few weeks before. As we entered the room, the first person I saw was none other than Tara Sivec, who was actually sitting in the hospital bed munching on a pack of Skittles.

"Hey ya, sis," she screeched, jumping up from the bed. In addition to the blue streak highlighting her brown hair, she was wearing a My Little Pony tank top that showed off the multiple tattoos on her arms, electric blue leggings, and four-inch stilettos. "It took you forever to get here. I was afraid you had the baby in the ambulance or something."

"Tell me about it," I mumbled gruffly. I was still overwhelmed with everything happening, and it was as if my brain was shut down from processing information, using all of its energy to overcome the God-awful pain ripping me apart.

If I wasn't already completely humiliated, the nurse asked "my sister" to help me change into the hospital gown while she got the bed ready. Flashing me her chipper little smile, Tara skipped over, proceeded to strip me, and then draped the flimsy fabric they called a gown across my front. When the nurse was finished with the bed, the two of them helped me into it, getting me situated and hooked up to all the machines.

"By the way, my name's Nancy," the friendly nurse finally introduced herself—not that I had time to wonder what her name was prior. "I've been assigned to you for the next nine hours, so let's see if we can get that baby to make its debut before I get off. Do you know what you're having?"

"One of each," I replied, trying my best to relax and catch my breath between contractions.

"Twins?!" they both exclaimed at the same time.

Tara quickly recovered as Nurse Nancy shot her a strange look. "Oh yes, we're so excited about the twins. Scarlett and I have always been so close; people used to joke we were like twins, not just...ya know...sisters," she explained, biting her lip to hide a giggle.

Nancy shrugged her shoulders and returned her focus to the machines. "Okay, Miss Scarlett, your doctor has been notified and will be here in a little while, but I'm going to check you now to see where you're at. Do you want your sister to stay in the room or leave for this?"

"I don't care; she can stay," I answered. I mean, shit, she'd already stripped me.

Nodding, she takes her place at the foot of the bed and warns me that it may be a bit uncomfortable. Funny, 'uncomfortable' would not have been the word I used to describe what she did to me—excruciating torture was more like it. My hips flew off the bed as I screamed out at her touch, and thankfully, she hastily withdrew her hand.

"You're progressing nicely. I'd say you're close to an eight and fully effaced—"

Her voice muffled as another contraction hit, and all I could focus on for the next sixty seconds was breathing my way through it while grabbing hold of the rails on the side of the bed.

"Do you know if she has a birthing plan?" I heard Nancy asking Tara as I came down from the pain, my eyes still closed.

"Yes, the plan is to push the babies out as pain-free as possible," my newly-adopted sister replied.

"So she does want an epidural?"

"Yes, our family is a huge proponent of drugs."

"I see. Well, let me put a call in to the anesthesiologist; she may be too far along already for it though. I'm honestly not sure her doctor's even going to make it in time."

I heard footsteps and the door closing, and I opened my eyes to stare at the textured ceiling, wondering what in the fuck was happening.

"I texted Mason; that's you're fiancé, right?" Tara said as she approached the bed.

Twisting my head to look at her, I nodded. "Yeah, thanks. How did you know?"

"I hope you don't mind; I went through your messages on your phone, but I figured you'd want him to know as soon as possible. You said something about it back at the signing," she explained. "He hasn't texted back yet."

"He's playing a show right now. He's gonna freak when he sees his phone."

"Well, it's a good thing I came then, girlie, 'cause according to the nurse lady, you're gonna be pushing these kiddos out pretty soon." She paused to sweep a few errant strands of hair away from my face. "And don't you worry—if you shit on the table while pushing, I won't tell a soul. Oh, and I'll make sure the doctor sews that shit up tight. Your boy, Mason, will think he's died and gone to virgin heaven once he can tap your cute ass again."

Speechless. Maybe I'd started to hallucinate and she really hadn't said that.

And as if the moment couldn't get any more ridiculous, the door flew open, and in walked the two other authors I completely humiliated myself in front earlier—Madeline and Ashley—both of them carrying boxes.

"We got here as soon as we could. It took us a while to get books signed from all of the authors for you, but here they are," one of them said. I didn't know who it was; I'd closed my eyes to pray I would disappear into the sheets. It was confirmed—I was starring in an episode of The Twilight Zone: Maternity Ward.

The three of them moved off to a corner and whispered between themselves for a few minutes until Nancy re-entered the room. "I see we have a couple new visitors. Hi, ladies, you must be more 'sisters'," she greeted them warmly, despite the hint of sarcasm lingering heavily on her last word.

After a murmur of hellos, Nancy then turned her attention to me. "Scarlett, I'm sorry to be the bearer of bad news, but I'm afraid you're going to have to do this without an epidural. Since you're having a vaginal delivery of twins, the on-call doctor doesn't want to impede the process in any way. He's going to be here in just a minute to check you himself, and most likely start setting everything up."

On cue, the door opened yet again, and in walked an older man dressed in baby blue scrubs, who reminded me of my grandpa. He introduced himself, and without even asking if I wanted anyone to leave the room, he began to check me. Thankfully, my "sisters" scurried up to the head of the bed so they weren't just standing there staring at my snatch.

Pulling the latex glove off his hand after the exam, he looked up at me and smiled. "It's time, sweetheart. We're gonna get everything ready, get our delivery team in here, and then we should be singing Happy Birthday to your little ones in just a bit. Everyone who isn't staying for the delivery should go ahead and move to the waiting room."

The following fifteen minutes were a whirlwind of motion, the room filling with hospital staff as they prepared for the twins' arrival. The contractions grew closer and closer together; I was having problems catching my breath in-between them. I thought the girls had left the room, and a part of me was a little sad; even though they were strangers, it'd meant a lot to me they had come to the hospital so I wouldn't be alone. However, as Nurse Nancy put the oxygen mask on my face, Tara appeared at the right side of the bed, picking my hand up to hold in hers.

"We're all here, sweetie. Let us know if we can do anything. Your man texted back and I've updated him; he's on his way," she comforted me.

And then it started.

Push... One – two – three – four – five – six – seven – eight – nine – ten. And rest.

Push... One – two – three – four – five – six – seven – eight – nine – ten. And rest.

Push... One – two – three – four – five – six – seven – eight – nine – ten. And rest.

Over and over and over.

I pushed so fucking hard I was afraid I was going to burst a blood vessel in my head.

Finally—and I mean holy-shitballs-fucking-FINALLY—the doctor told me one last push and the first baby would be out. Bearing down with every ounce of oomph left in me, Everett Matthew entered the world on February seventh at six-thirty-two in the evening. Three minutes later, his partner-in-crime,

Ashlynn Marley, followed, and the room of strangers erupted into cheers. Both babies were whisked away to be cleaned, measured, and examined, and once I was told they were both breathing on their own and screaming loudly, I passed out cold.

The sound of the toilet flushing startles me, and I leap to my feet, snatching my water bottle and leaving the barrage of pictures scattered about. Scurrying to the bedroom, I bound into the room just as Mason exits the bathroom.

"Where were you, Angel?" he asks groggily, walking back to the bed, still stark naked. I clench my thighs together at the sight of him; he truly is a specimen.

"I went to get some water and got sidetracked unpacking a box." Crawling onto the mattress simultaneously, I meet him in the middle with a quick kiss.

Growling, he grabs the bottom hem of my t-shirt and yanks it over my head. "And you put clothes on. I want you naked. It's not time for unpacking."

I promptly slide the panties down my legs and toss them to the floor before he rips them off. Clutching my hips, he rolls onto his back and pulls me on top of him in one swift motion. "Better," he mumbles, reaching up to cup my breasts, both thumbs playfully brushing back and forth over my nipples. "Don't make me handcuff you to the bed," he teases.

Looking at all of the old pictures and remembering what it was like when I was pregnant and delivered the twins ignited a desire inside of me. It's something the two of us discussed several times, but the timing was never right; however, now that we're married and in our own home, I'm ready.

Wiggling on top of his cock pressing into the cleft of my ass, I lift my arms and gather my hair in a messy pile on top of my head, doing the best sexy-seductress-Scarlett I can. "Mase, I'm ready," I rasp.

"Fuck right, you're ready, baby." He grinds his hips against me, provoking a guttural moan from the back of my throat.

I splay my hands across his sinfully-sexy chest, staring deeply into his lustful eyes. "I want another baby."

Chapter Eight

Our Kind of Crazy

(Home ~ Phillip Phillips)

SCARLETT

The scorching, bright rays of the morning sun cut through the bedroom window way too early, shining directly into my sleep-deprived eyes only a couple of hours after Mason and I had way too much fun 'trying' to make another baby. Hiding my head under the pillow, I silently curse myself for not making him hang the damn curtains last night.

"Morning, beautiful," he says in his sleepy voice from the other side of the bed.

I grunt my displeasure at him without moving. Lifting the fluffy shield from my head, he rolls me onto my back and kisses the top of my forehead. His head is propped up by his elbow, and he's smiling down at me adoringly. "Someone's grumpy this morning," he teases, tickling my bare belly with his free hand. You can't be pregnant already, right?"

Chuckling, I roll my eyes and shake my head. "No, silly, I'm still on birth control; I can't be pregnant yet. I'm grouchy because I'm still sleepy and the sun is blinding me."

He repositions himself to block the light from my face. "But you did mean what you said? You want to have another baby?"

I can't tell if he's hoping I did or didn't mean it—or maybe a little of both. Nervously, I nibble on my bottom lip and nod my head. "Yeah, I know we've talked about having more, but I didn't want to until we were off the bus permanently and settled. As many great memories we made with the kids traveling all over the world the last few years, I don't want to do it again."

"We were pretty crazy, weren't we?" His warm laugh intoxicates me, and I'm thankful we can joke about our not-so-conventional way of raising a family.

"Yes, we were—and sometimes still are," I reply softly, reaching up to tenderly trace my finger over his morning stubble. "We're always a good crazy though."

Grasping my hand, he kisses my palm then abruptly sits up, the gray sheet pooling around his waist. "Speaking of kids and crazy, we need to get up and get busy. They'll be home tomorrow night and this place is a wreck."

"Okay, I promise I'll get busy, but I want to show you something first. Let's get dressed and make some coffee."

Fifteen minutes later, Mason and I—each holding a piping hot mug—are sitting on the living room floor surrounded by the photos I've been reminiscing over for the past day. I show him all the ones I've been through thus far, and we laugh over most of the memories. I notice his eyes get a little glossy when he sees the pictures with the authors holding the babies. He'd been extremely upset he wasn't there when they were born.

Reaching into the storage bin, I pull out another set—ones of him and the twins—and a huge grin stretches across his face. It was the day he introduced the world to Everett and Ashlynn.

No amount of reading, searching websites, or listening to other parents could've prepared me for what life with newborn twins would be like. Holy fucking shit—and I mean that exactly how it sounds.

The babies and I were both released from the hospital three days after their birth. They both weighed-in at just over five pounds and had no health issues whatsoever, so they sent us all on our merry way—no instructions, no handbook, just a stack of papers explaining what we owed. Mason brought us to our makeshift home of a hotel suite, and we literally looked at each other and said, "What next?"

Sophie pretty much moved in with us for the first few weeks until we figured everything out and developed somewhat of a schedule. It took us nearly a month, but eventually, I became proactive instead of reactive; I began to anticipate their needs and was prepared. Mason was amazing with the babies, always asking what he could do to help or watching them while I rested. He often felt bad because he'd be gone ten or more hours during the day as they recorded their third album with the new producer, but I understood they had a specific timeframe to get it all done before leaving for the third tour. Thankfully, Sophie continued to come over daily to help me out.

The third tour—that's when things got really interesting.

Owen arranged for Mason, the twins, and me to have our own smaller bus that followed the larger one while we traveled throughout the states. I offered time and time again to stay in California or move back to the apartment in Houston until the tour was over, but Mason wouldn't hear of it. He refused to be apart from me and the babies for any length of time, so when the twins were five months old, we packed up our family and moved onto our little bus for a six-month stint on the road. Crazy as shit.

The night of their opening performance in San Francisco, I was completely caught off-guard when Mason asked me to bring the twins on stage, and the band then closed the show with a cover of "A Father's First Spring" by The Avett Brothers. Pride soared through me with such intensity I was afraid my heart would explode. I couldn't have asked for a better father for my children, or a better caretaker of my heart.

Over the next several months, we learned how to live as a family on the road. Some days were harder than others, but as long as we were all together, we were home. Before Ashlynn and Everett turned one, they'd crossed the Golden Gate Bridge, seen the Grand Canyon, stood under the Gateway Arch, and had even been to the top of the Empire State Building. Our family had been interviewed by TV shows such as Ellen and The Talk—everyone always wondering how in the world we managed two infants in the confines of a bus. I'm not sure we even knew; we just made it work.

The US portion of the tour wrapped up in mid-January, giving us ten days off before we travelled overseas. It was the first time the twins actually stayed in our true home in Houston. While we were gone, Andi and Mina had transformed the spare bedroom into a nursery for them, which was absolutely breathtaking. Walking into the room, I felt as if I'd been transported into a serene rainforest; sage green bedding, trees painted on the walls, a sound machine playing nature sounds...they'd thought of everything. Unfortunately, ten days was just long enough to get used to being back before we had to leave yet again.

Our ten weeks in Europe and Asia was extremely challenging, yet exceptionally rewarding. Flying from place to place and hopping from hotel to hotel—often not speaking the native tongue—with the babies was much more difficult than being on the bus. We could only take with us what would fit in suitcases, which meant no swings, exersaucers, or anything else to keep them from crawling around and getting into everything, and most of the hotel rooms we stayed in were not infant-friendly, to say the least.

On the upside, we got to experience these foreign cities on a first-class ticket. Many of the places I'd dreamed of visiting were a part of the tour—London, Paris, Venice, Moscow, Frankurt, and the list went on. We celebrated the twins' first birthday atop the Eiffel Tower—something they'll never remember, but I'll never forget. They both took their first steps in foreign countries—Everett in Germany, and Ashlynn in Spain. One off-night while we were in Italy, Sophie and Aaron kept the babies overnight to give Mase and me a much-needed break and alone time. We had dinner at a fancy Italian restaurant, followed by a ride down the canal on the famous gondolas, and with big plans of a long night filled with hot sex...we both fell asleep before midnight. Thankfully though, we became masters of utilizing the kids' nap times wisely to fit in our sexcapades. I had more sex in hotel room bathrooms than I ever dreamed possible. We did what we had to do in order to keep the spark alive, and through it all, our relationship grew stronger and more resilient, and our love matured and flourished.

Glancing over at Mason as we get to the end of the stack of pictures—a year of our life summed up in photographs—I see the memories affecting him the same way they have me.

"Crazy. It seems like just yesterday, but so long ago at the same time," he murmurs, still gazing at a photo of the four of us standing in front of the Sagrada Familia Cathedral.

I rest my head on his shoulder, sighing softly. "Always a good crazy."

Chapter Nine

Giving It Up

(You Still Love Me ~ Tyrone Wells)

MASON

Damn Scarlett and her good distractions. I know we really need to get to work unpacking all these damn boxes, but between her tempting me with that sexy-as-fuck body, and getting me lost in the memories of the two little ones I cherish more than anything in the world, I'm not being very productive. The three of them have introduced me to a life I never knew I wanted, and now couldn't live without. Growing up with less-than-spectacular parents, before I met Scarlett, I had no intention of ever settling down with one woman, much less having a family. I never wanted to disappoint anyone the way my parents did me. But once I fell for her, I knew I'd do whatever it took to make her happy, and as fucking pussy-whipped as that makes me sound, I don't give a rat's ass—full pun intended.

Our journey to this point hasn't always been good—shit, it was downright God-awful at times in the beginning—but here we are, our love stronger than I ever could've imagined. It's hard to believe it was over eight years ago when my dark-haired, green-eyed beauty walked into my bar, exuding an innocence that first captured my attention, and later stole my heart. There's no point in rehashing the ways we fucked up or the choices we made; it all happened the way it was supposed to in order to get us to this place. Happiness.

Looking at all the pictures from the past six years, I'm reminded of our trek here, and if I had it to do all over again, I wouldn't change a thing. Many people don't realize it, but Scarlett sacrificed a lot to make our relationship work. When she left to go on tour with me, she gave up the notion of going back to school and stopped playing her own music, stepping into a life of attention-starved whores and headline-hungry journalists that stripped her of her privacy. Yet she never complained. Not fucking once. She gave up everything so I could pursue my dream, always there when I needed a reassuring word, always there when I needed to fuck away my frustrations, and always there to support me unconditionally.

When I strongly suggested that she and the twins go on tour with me—probably for more selfish reasons than I'd like to admit—she was onboard. I know life like that wasn't easy, especially for her since she was with the babies twenty-four-seven, but she did it so we could be together. Then for the next three and a half years, as the babies grew into toddlers, she continued to travel with me, always just because I asked her to.

I'll never forget the day I decided to give it all up, which turned out to be the best decision of my life. We were in New York a week after my twenty-ninth birthday, and I'd gone out for an early-morning run. As I passed by a newsstand, a picture on the front of a magazine caught my eye. Immediately, I stopped cold. It was a photo of Everett and Ashlynn skipping down a sidewalk while holding Scarlett's hands. The headline read: *Traveling Tots: Life on the Road with Twins.* I purchased the magazine, and then found the closest bench to sit down and read the article. The entire piece was very flattering, complimenting Scarlett on how she's managed to raise the kids while always on the go. I'm not sure what it was exactly, but something inside of me changed at that moment. Call it a wakeup call, a slap in the face, a turning point—whatever the fuck you want, all that matters is everything was different. As much as I loved music and performing, I loved my family exponentially more, and suddenly it became so obvious to me—I'd been so greedy and so self-centered to have them make such sacrifices, but they went along with it just to make me happy.

That night, we performed at Madison Square Garden, and I couldn't wait to get off the stage and back to my family in the hotel. Suddenly, as if my rose-colored glasses had been stripped away, I saw everyone around me for what they really were—users and abusers. Other than my bandmates and a few select others, all of the people surrounding me didn't care about what the best thing for me was, nor did they didn't give two shits about my family. Their only concern was how I could help them improve their own lives.

As soon as I returned to the room, I woke everyone up—I hadn't cared what time it was—and informed them of the decision I'd come to. The twins were really too young to understand, but they cheered anyway because I seemed so excited. Scarlett was hesitant to show any emotion, confused over why I'd had a change of heart and, as usual, putting my feelings first. I promised her I was one hundred percent confident in my decision; as soon as the current tour we were on was complete, I was finished. Done. Terminado. Finito. I wanted to give Scarlett the wedding and marriage she deserved, the kids the stability they needed, and for the four of us to enjoy the life we were blessed with.

It's been almost a year since that day, and not one single moment have I regretted it.

"Come on, Angel. This has been fun, but we really need to get busy," I say, looking over at the empty space she'd been sitting in. I scan the room, but she's nowhere to be found. "Hey, where'd you go?"

Her hearty laughter echoes throughout the house. "I'm in here," she calls out from the kitchen. "You were so lost in your thoughts you didn't even hear me when I told you I was coming in here to unpack."

Strolling through the archway that separates the two rooms, I hiss under my breath at the sight of her lithe body bent over putting away pots and pans—a body I'll never be able to get enough of. Her black lace panties peek out of the cotton sleep-shirt she's still wearing, and my cock twitches to life with the need to feel myself buried deep inside her yet again. *Never fucking enough.*

My legs move of their own accord, positioning me directly behind her so I can encase my arms around her tiny waist and press my erection against her ass. "You're being good like you promised, I see."

Setting down the skillet in her hands, she peeks over her shoulder at me, her lips curling up in a smirk. "I'm *always* good," she replies with a shake of her hips.

She knows better than to test my resolve. For someone who prides himself in self-control—a vital attribute when it comes to sustaining a successful relationship while in the music business—I have no fucking willpower when it comes to her and her mind-blowing curves. Without another word, I hook my thumbs into the sides of her panties, push them past her hipbones, and let them fall to the floor. A seductive moan rumbles deep in her throat, fueling my need for her even more—as if that's possible.

"Hold on to the countertop," I growl hoarsely.

Immediately, her hands fly up and grasp the black granite surface, presenting her perfectly-shaped ass to me. She's just as ready to take as I am to give, our voracious libidos always on the same page.

With one of my hands splayed across her ivory cheeks, the other brushes a feathery-light stroke across her already-wet folds. Her breath hitches on contact as she tries to grind her body harder against my hand. I withdraw it and slap her firmly across the butt. "Be patient or I'll really torture you," I warn wickedly.

Part of me wants her to disobey so I can spend the next few hours tormenting her supple body, driving her to the edge over and over without letting her free-fall into her orgasm until I determine she's had enough, but her body stills, so I return my nimble fingers back to her glistening sex. Again, I barely graze her puffy lips with my fingertips, sweeping up and down several times until I realize she's going to behave. Then, after dipping my middle digit into her tight slit, I drag it towards her front, coating her hardened clit with her own juices as I make small circular motions against it.

"Fuck, Mase. You're killing me," she mutters breathlessly. She's trying desperately not to move, allowing me my naughty playtime with her irresistibly enticing body.

Luckily for her, I can't take much more myself; my steel-hard cock is throbbing with hunger, and only her wrapping tightly around me will satisfy my craving. Withdrawing my hand from her swollen nub, I hastily pull my boxers down and align the tip of my shaft—already oozing with pre-cum—at her entrance, grasping both of her hips to keep her steady. Her fingers tighten around the curved edge of the counter, bracing herself for what she knows is coming.

Plunging deep inside her with one swift thrust, her tight walls stretch around my width, allowing me to completely immerse myself in her gripping, tight, searing-hot pussy. I draw back until only the head is still hidden in her slit—the sheen from her arousal covering my erection—before burying myself into her again. Over and over, I drive my cock into her molten core, digging my short nails into her creamy, soft flesh as I propel us to the height of our desire.

Our sweaty bodies slap thunderously against each other. The heady smell of sex hangs dense in the air like cumulonimbus clouds blanketing the sky. Electric currents whirr with lightning-fast speed between our bodies. We soar higher and higher, the storm within us growing more intense with every movement until the passionate tempest claims both of our bodies. Together, we burst free, flooding each other with our all-consuming orgasm until we're both fully-drained and sated.

Looping my arms around her slender frame, I pull her down with me as I collapse onto the floor, my legs no longer able to hold me up. Nuzzling the nape of her neck, I hold her back flush against my chest and whisper, "You are fucking crazy."

She tilts her head back on my shoulder so she can look at me, sensual satisfaction swimming in her bright emerald eyes as she grins impishly. "Always a good crazy."

Chapter Ten

Timeless Memories

(Crazy Love ~ Van Morrison)
ONE MONTH LATER

SCARLETT

Our hope of having the house unpacked and ready to go before the twins came home over that long weekend quickly proved to be a pipe dream, especially when Mason and I couldn't keep our hands off of each other or our clothes on for any period of time. We quickly accepted our failed expectations, and instead, we spent the time without kids having a second honeymoon of sorts, christening every room downstairs in less than forty-eight hours.

In all actuality, it took us a little over a week to get all of the boxes unpacked and everything set up precisely the way I wanted. I'm still adding decorative touches to each of the rooms, which is apparently a never-ending project that continues to evolve as I go. I may buy stock in Hobby Lobby and Pier One shortly with as much money as I'm regularly dumping at both of those stores.

Today, I'm working in the game room, while Mase and the kids are outside swimming. Knowing I need to shower and start getting all of us ready for dinner soon, the last thing I'll have time to finish is choosing some photos for the funky, animal-print frames I found last week. Searching through the storage closet underneath the staircase, I can't find the bin with all of the photos we'd spent hours sifting through that initial weekend.

Sauntering through the house, I open the backdoor and call out, "Hey, babe, have you moved that container with all of the pictures? I thought I put it under the stairs, right?"

Three amused faces bob up and down in the shallow end of the pool amidst brilliant prisms produced by the sunlight reflecting off of the rippling water. A huge smile spreads across my face at the sight of them, overjoyed with how much our time together as a family has been enhanced in the short time we've lived in the house.

"No, I haven't moved it. Are you sure it's not in there?"

"Yeah, I've looked everywhere," I reply with a shrug. "Oh well, no biggie. I'll search for it later. Y'all need to get out soon so we can get dressed if we're going to make dinner on time. I'm going to jump in the shower now." A bunch of splashing and laughing ensues as I hear all three of them yell "yes, ma'am" out to me before I close the door.

An hour-and-a-half later, the four of us load into our black Tahoe and head into the city for my birthday celebration with our closest friends and family. Twenty-seven years young. It's hard to believe it'd been nearly nine years since I left my parents' restrictive home, naïve, innocent, and unaware of the raw emotions connected with love and loss. Looking over at my husband and kids as we drive down the highway, my heart clenches with gratitude and love. Despite the sorrow I will always carry over losing both Evie and Ash, I know I'm truly blessed.

Pulling into the parking lot of Empty's—which is closed to the public for the night—the kids scurry out of the SUV as soon as it's in park, rushing inside to play air hockey with their Uncle Marcus. Smiling, Mase and I walk hand-in-hand through the heavy metal door, instantly surrounded by our loved ones. There are more people than I expected in attendance, and I glance over at my husband with a raised brow, silently scolding him for making this bigger than necessary. A tender kiss on my forehead is the only response I get.

Everyone seems to be having a great time; the barbeque on the buffet has been devoured, people are laughing and joking while playing pool and darts, and several of us can't stop ourselves from dancing to the mixture of classic rock and Top 40 hits booming through the speakers. Someone announces it's time to sing *Happy Birthday* and eat cake, so everyone gathers together near the stage, placing me in the center. Confusion sets in when a huge white screen I didn't even know existed descends from the ceiling and the lights dim. Looking around for Mase, he's nowhere to be found, until he strolls out on stage a few minutes later holding his acoustic. *I'm going to kill him when we get home.* His eyes meet mine, sparkling with mischief, and he shakes his head at me as if he knows my last thought.

"Good evening, everyone," he says warmly into the microphone. "I know most of us have all been together recently for our wedding, but I really wanted to do something special for my wife to show her how much I appreciate everything she's done for me and our family. I'm pretty sure her last six or seven birthdays have been spent on the road with the band, and definitely didn't get the attention they deserved, so I've put together a little something to remind her of our journey here."

As he begins to strum his guitar, a video appears on the screen behind him. The first shot is a collage of miscellaneous Polaroid pictures, with a quote reading, *"Memories are timeless treasures of the heart."* Then, a steady flow of photographs from the past six-plus years—the ones we had laughed and cried over on our recent trip down Memory Lane—streams across the screen. Happy tears fill my eyes, not only at the reminiscent images, but at the awe-inspiring thoughtfulness he put into having this made for me.

"I can hear her heart beat for a thousand miles,
And the heavens open every time she smiles..."

When he begins to sing *Crazy Love* by Van Morrison, I can no longer hold back the emotions bubbling over, and so the waterworks begin. Feverishly, I try to wipe the moisture from my eyes and swallow back the sob lodged in the back of my throat so I don't miss any of the video. He's covered it all—our last first kiss at the homecoming celebration, leaving together on tour, the romantic proposal, the lengthy pregnancy, the twins' birth and all of the ridiculousness surrounding it, our family traveling all over the world, and finally, the wedding of my dreams. The last image on the screen is one of us outside at our reception, Everett in my arms and Ashlynn in his, and all four of us are staring up into the dusk-kissed sky, mesmerized by the hundreds of butterflies fluttering around us.

Calling me up on stage to stand next to him, he sings the chorus one last time while staring into the depths of my soul through my glassy eyes.

"She give me love, love, love, love, crazy love

She give me love, love, love, love, crazy love"

Standing on my tiptoes, I press my lips to his in a tender yet overwhelmingly meaningful kiss and then whisper, "Always a good crazy."

The End

When the Sun Goes Down, a new series by Erin Noelle, is now available on Amazon, Barnes & Noble, Kobo, and iBooks. Enjoy the first two chapters here.

When the Sun Goes Down

PROLOGUE

Eight Years Prior

"We the jury, find the defendant, Robert Allen Green, *not guilty* in the sole count of the crime of murder in the first degree."

The words *not guilty* echo throughout the courtroom like a shot in the night. Everyone is stunned to silence, including the man on trial and his team of attorneys. The young, teenaged girl sitting in the front row jumps up, tears streaming wildly down her face as she screams, "I saw him do it! I watched him kill my mom with my own eyes! How can this happen? What is wrong with you people?"

The judge bangs his gavel and calls for order in the court, while the adults surround the girl, pick her up, and carry her out of the courtroom. Right before they get her through the door, she turns over her shoulder and calls out in a choked sob. "*You* will pay for this! I will get revenge!"

Chapter One

Trina

(Mysterious Ways ~ U2)

"Miss Foster! Miss Foster! Is today puh-cussion day?"

"Miss Foster, can I play the bongo drums?"

"No, I want to play the bongos, Josie! Girls play the triangle!"

"Paul, you should play the bells, 'cause you're a ding dong."

Chuckling to myself at the last comment, I attempt to get the class under control. "Okay, boys and girls, everyone take a seat on a colored circle and calm down. There will be plenty of opportunities for each of you to play all of the instruments today." I don't scold Josie for calling him a ding dong, even though I should; I have a hard time reprimanding students who speak the truth. Thankfully, all of the children listen and do as they're told, without even an argument about who sits on which color.

I look around at their eager seven-year-old faces and my heart is filled with warmth. I love my job. The innocence of childhood is one of the few things that still brings joy to my life. Music is another... if only I could spend all of my days, here in the classroom, surrounded by these two untarnished things in my life. Unfortunately, that's not the case, but I make sure to soak up every moment while I'm here. Turning my attention to the ten or so instruments I've set out for today's lesson, I begin the hour long class.

Three classes later - all of which are second graders today - it's time for lunch. I make my way down the hall to the teacher's lounge and grab my food out of the refrigerator. My leftovers from the night before are almost finished heating up, when I hear an all too familiar voice screech behind me.

"Trina Foster! There you are, woman!" Her arms slip around my waist as she hugs my back, and I flinch just a bit.

"Hiya, Lauren. How's your morning?" I ask, pulling my chicken and rice out of the microwave. I turn around to face her cute little freckled face and can tell by her expression that it hasn't been a good one. "Uh oh, what's wrong?"

She motions for me to follow her to one of the sofas. We both plop down after I set my food on the table nearest to me. "First, tell me about your spring break. Did you do anything fun? Go on any hot dates?" she asks hopefully.

I shake my head and laugh. "Boring, no, and no. Okay, your turn. What or who has got you all upset today?"

"Oh, just a bunch of shit. I found out that prick Jason is dating like four other girls, my rent is increasing a couple hundred dollars when my lease is up in the summer, I'm so pathetic I spent the majority of the week off at my parents' house, and my kids are refusing to listen today." She flashes a big, cheesy, fake smile at me. "So not much, really."

I push my glasses up on my nose a bit and tilt my head at her. "Screw Jason, find a new place to live, be thankful you have parents to visit, and they're kids; be patient. It's the first day back after vacation." Smiling sweetly at her, I take a bite of my lunch.

"Well, don't you have all the answers? I think I'll just call you Alex Trebek," she teases, then takes a long slurp from her diet shake thing that she always drinks for lunch.

"No, no. I don't look like an Alex at all. I could never pull that off – my boobs prevent me from being a boy-Alex and I'm not nearly exotic enough to be a girl-Alex," I reply deadpan.

We both burst out laughing to the point I think she's going to choke on her drink. Everyone in the room looks at us like we are crazy, and I immediately get quiet. I hate to bring attention to myself here at work. I don't need anyone passing judgment on me or assuming they know anything about me. I'd prefer they not think about me at all.

"Shh, Lauren, people are staring," I urge her to stop making a scene.

"Oh, who cares, Trina?" she asks waving her hand in the air. "They're all a bunch of old fogeys. We really need to get you to loosen up some."

I simply shake my head and gather up my containers, leaving her sitting on the couch to go throw my trash away. We've had this conversation way too many times, and I really don't want to do it again today.

"You are nearly twenty three years old. You need a life outside your job. It's not healthy," she hisses into my ear a few seconds later. "Come out with me tonight or one day this week... just one drink and we will be home early."

Groaning, I turn around and stare at her, my face expressionless. "I appreciate your concern for my health, but my primary care physician, gynecologist, and psychologist all seem to think that I'm just fine. I like my life the way it is - easy and drama-free. Now, if you'll excuse me, I have a classroom of budding musicians waiting for me."

I walk past her, leaving her standing there, mouth wide open. I don't want to be rude to one of my only friends, I don't like to hurt people's feelings, but I don't know any other way to get her off my back about my social life. No one understands.

As I grab the door knob to exit the lounge, she calls out, "I'm not giving up, Trina! I will break you eventually!" I pause for a moment, closing my eyes and shaking my head. I contemplate turning around and saying something back, but I'm sure we have an audience at this point. Instead, I turn the knob and push the door open... right into someone's face.

"Crap! That hurt!" I hear a male voice say seconds after I feel the door make contact.

"Oh my goodness! I'm so sorry!" I squeak as I move to see my victim.

Standing there - holding his nose as blood streams out like he just climbed out of an MMA octagon - is a guy around my age, that I've never seen before, dressed in khakis and a white polo.

"You're bleeding! Oh, I feel awful! I'm so sorry; I didn't know you were standing there," I squeak out an apology, unsure of what to do.

He laughs softly and I bring my eyes to meet his. They are the most unusual eyes I have ever seen – one is sky blue, while the other is a light brown. In any other circumstances, I would comment on the uniqueness of it, but right now I'm too flustered. When he speaks to me, I look away, realizing that I've been staring. "I should hope not, or I'd be really offended."

"Excuse me?" I ask.

"I hope you didn't know I was standing there and hit me on purpose," he explains. "Then, I may think you don't like me."

I blush and continue to keep my gaze far from his. "I don't know if I like you or not; I don't know you. I've never seen you around here before."

"That would be because today is my first day here. I'm taking over for Ms. Jordan who's on maternity leave for the rest of the year. Ya know, I would love to continue this conversation at a different time when I could actually shake your hand and not be covering my face, but I should probably clean up and get some ice on this," he says, his voice softening a bit.

I nod my head. "I'm sorry again about your nose and your shirt. If you bring it to me I can get those stains out for you."

He looks down at the blood stains on his shoulder and chest, and instead of getting angry or frustrated, he laughs. "Okay, Miss; I'm sorry I didn't get your name."

"Miss Foster," I reply quickly, still looking down at the ground. "And I really should go, my kids will be waiting."

"Yes ma'am, Miss Foster. I'll take you up on that offer." I nod again and raise my head up to his chest level, so it doesn't appear that I'm completely rude. "My name is Lucca, or Mr. Ellis, if we're sticking with last names. And despite the circumstances, it was a pleasure to meet you." I hear the playful tone in his voice; he knows I'm embarrassed, but he's trying not to make me feel more uncomfortable.

Spinning on my heel, I hurry back to my classroom and try desperately to forget about the lunch encounter over the remainder of the afternoon classes. The kids make it easy to get lost in their excitement over beating on some drums and making as much noise as possible. It's not often they get to do this without getting yelled at about it. When the final bell rings a little after three o'clock, I say goodbye to my last class of the day and begin to clean up the room. Being Monday, it's hot yoga day, and I'm really looking forward to a session of sweaty planks, downward dogs, and cobras.

I'm bent over putting away the last of the drums when I hear someone clear their throat at the door. I sigh aloud, assuming that it's Lauren, and without turning around, I say, "I'm not going out with you tonight or any other night. It's just not happening. Ever."

"Our initial introduction wasn't ideal, I agree, but I think you're being rather harsh," that same throaty voice that had danced in my ears earlier in the day retorts.

Snapping upright and turning around sharply, my entire face enflames. "Oh my goodness, Lucca, or uh Mr. Ellis, I'm so sorry... again." I shake my head, hardly believing what an idiot I can be. "I thought you were someone else. I didn't mean to be so rude. I wouldn't say that... I mean, it's not that I *do* want to... I mean, I didn't..." I just stop talking since nothing is coming out right.

He continues to stand in the doorway, grinning like a fool, obviously enjoying the fact that I'm rattled. "You were saying?" he asks.

Now that he's not covering his face, I can't help but to notice how handsome he is... even with the bandage on his nose and the beginnings of a black eye. His hair is as dark as mine is light and he's got that style where it's sticking up every which way, like he just rolled out of bed, yet it still looks perfect. He's got the kind of smile that makes most girls go weak in the knees. Thank God, I'm not most girls. I mentally pull myself together to find my voice and my inner calm.

"I apologize for those remarks; I honestly thought you were someone else. And again, I'm sorry for the collision earlier," I say softly. "I'm usually not so rude as to give someone a black eye and verbally accost them within the first day of meeting. Now, what is it that brings you by this afternoon?"

He leisurely walks over to where I stand, smirking the entire way. I don't like the way he makes me feel, and I really don't like the way he's looking at me right now. "Well, Miss Foster, if I remember correctly, you offered to take care of my shirt for me." He pauses and pulls the shirt over his head, leaving him standing in just his pants less than three feet from me. Instinctively, my eyes are drawn to his tight chest and abs like fingers to a cello; his torso is perfect instrumentally. I force myself to pull my stare up to his face, to those exquisite eyes. He's still got that shit-eating grin on his face, and he knows exactly what he's doing. He holds the shirt out to me and I snatch it from his hands.

"I'll return it to you soon," I force out in my sweetest possible voice and then turn away to walk towards my desk. I don't want to give him the satisfaction of knowing that he's getting to me. I hear his footsteps walking towards the door, but before he leaves, he calls out, "Yes ma'am, Miss Foster, I'll see you tomorrow."

My entire body flinches at his words.

Chapter Two

Kat

(The Only Time — Nine Inch Nails)

Drying off after my nightly bubble bath, I lather up my freshly shaved, now extremely smooth skin in my favorite Kanebo Sensai body cream. My skin feels like pure silk and smells like a whiff of heaven after I apply it from head to toe. There truly is no other lotion or cream on the market that is even close to this stuff. I'm not sure what it is about it, but something in the plants and extracts that they use, make it worth every dollar I spend on it - all four hundred of them.

I slide into my black, silk robe, not even bothering with the tie that dangles around my waist, and make my way to the kitchen. I grab the open bottle of 2011 Chevalier-Montrachet out of the wine chiller and pour myself a healthy glass. After the first sip of the expressive chardonnay, my taste buds come to life and I moan aloud in delight. The hint of spicy floral mixed with a zest of lemon is an impeccable combination, and much like my lotion, is irreplaceable in my nightly ritual.

Leisurely making my way back to my bedroom with my vino, I saunter into my closet to decide what I'm going to wear tonight. Typically, I wear all black on Monday's, but after the day I've had, I'm feeling a little like breaking the rules tonight - even if they are my own rules. Shaking my head and laughing softly at myself, I grab my new sapphire-blue fitted dress off of it's hanger with a pair of silver stilettos and throw them on my oversized bed.

I head back into the bathroom and climb up on the marble countertop, yelping as my bare ass hits the cold surface. I have to sit up here to put my make up on; it's like it doesn't apply correctly if I don't. It's similar to when I have to fix my hair standing in front of the left sink instead of the right. There's a certain way and order that everything needs to be done in, otherwise my inner balance gets thrown off and I spin a little out of control, and nobody wants that to happen.

Smiling at myself in the mirror, I begin to apply the dark charcoal eyeliner that frames my crystal blue eyes, then I follow it up with several thick coats of mascara. I'm blessed that I have naturally long lashes and don't have to go through the trouble of falsies; unfortunately, they are just very pale, like everything else on me. After a little blush and all over shimmery powder, I overlay my naturally ruby lips with a thin coat of cherry lip gloss and blow myself a kiss in the mirror. Seriously, who could resist this face?

I hop off of the counter and move over to the hair station, bringing my now half-finished glass of wine with me. I release my long flaxen blonde hair from the clip that's been holding it on top of my head, allowing it to cascade down my back. Thirty minutes with the straightener and I'm good to go. I stare at my reflection one last time before turning to get dressed. Perfect ~ just enough make up to accent my eyes and lips and my hair looks better than Duchess Catherine's. I have mastered the concept of sexy without slutty. People have always told me that I have the face of a porcelain doll, and truly, I must agree. Unfortunately for them, I share the same emotional capacity as one of those dolls in my bitter, frozen heart.

I take off the robe, hang it in its designated spot on the back of the bathroom door, and then prance naked over to my wardrobe to choose my lingerie for the evening. This is probably my favorite part of the entire getting ready process. A woman's undergarments truly say so much about her mood and intentions. For example, a woman in a white cotton bra and panties probably isn't thinking about getting fucked, and even if she is, she doesn't care much about impressing her partner. Whereas a lady in sheer black lace is at least hoping that someone will get a peek at her without clothes on. The fabric and color of my intimate apparel most definitely affects my attitude and disposition; plus, it's the basis on which an entire outfit is built around.

Seeing that I'm completely going against my better judgment and wearing blue and silver tonight, I opt for my grey metallic demi cup bra with the matching thong. Sitting on my bed, I carefully slide my iridescent thigh highs up my perfectly toned legs and hook them to the grey garters. Stockings and garters are a must for me anytime I leave home after sunset. This is one rule that *can't* be broken. When I slide the sleek, delicate material onto my body and attach it to the clasps that perfectly frame my tight ass and sweet pussy, a switch goes off in my head - a switch that locks away any sliver of goodness left in my soul and turns me into a fierce predator with only one goal in mind ~ to dominate and destroy.

I glance at the clock and see that it's a few minutes past ten, which means that I need to get a move on. I quickly slip into my dress and shoes, then take one last look at myself in the full length mirror. I should feel bad for the men who cross my path tonight. Too bad I don't. I swallow down the last of my drink as I walk towards the front of the apartment. Stopping to rinse out my glass and placing it in the dishwasher, I then grab my clutch off the table and head out the front door.

Emerging from the elevator, I give Andres, the nightly security guard, a quick smile and tip of my head, before escaping into the cool March night. Leo is waiting for me with the SUV, just as he is every night, and I hurry into the backseat of the black Range Rover. He closes the door behind me and hurries around to slide in the driver's seat.

"Where are we headed tonight, Miss Kat?" he asks as we pull away from my building.

"The World Bar Trump Towers. I'm feeling feisty tonight and need some international blood." I reply in a sharp tone. He glances up into the rear view mirror and catches my eye. His expression speaks volumes, but he's smart enough to not say anything.

I raise my eyebrows at him. "Do you notice anything different about me tonight, Leo?"

"You're not wearing black, Miss Kat," he says without even having to think.

"You're always so observant. I really don't pay you enough."

"You pay me more than enough, but thank you for the compliment."

He smiles at me in the mirror, and I allow myself to return the friendly gesture. Being in his presence calms me like no other. He is the only male in my life that I never intentionally want to hurt, but I know that I still do. Daily. Our relationship is unconventional and most definitely unhealthy. He is the closest thing I know to love, yet it's still so fucked up that I'm not even sure that's the correct terminology for it. I know he loves me, and I care about him as much as I can, but that's not saying much.

Before I can spend any more time thinking about Leo, we pull up to the building and he hops out of the car to come open my door. I take his offered hand and slide down off of the black leather seat. As my feet hit the ground, I give him a quick peck on the cheek. "This shouldn't take long," I tell him, and he simply nods knowingly. I stride confidently though the door, and once inside, I scan the room swiftly before making my way to the lit up marble bar. Every person present, both male and female, watches as I make my way across the room. I feel their eyes on me, and instead of making me uncomfortable as it would many people, I feed off the attention.

The bar is quite crowded for a Monday, which pleases me immensely - more of a menu to choose from. I select the open chair in between two men who both appear to be there alone. The one on the left is a little old for my liking, but the one on the right caught my eye immediately. The bartender, dressed in his white tux, scurries to greet me.

"What can I get for you to drink this evening, ma'am?"

"Grey Goose Martini. Dry, dirty, and with a twist, please." He nods his head with a smile and steps away to make my drink.

"There's nothing sexier than a beautiful woman who knows how to order a drink," the older gentleman says to me. I refrain from rolling my eyes and swallow back the words that I want to say. It's time to play the game.

I look over at Grandpa and grin. "How sweet of you to call me beautiful; thank you so much." One good look at his face and I know that even if his age didn't rule him out, his uni-brow would've. Thankfully, the bartender arrives with my drink at the perfect time to end this conversation that's barely started. I thank him and take a sip of the cocktail. Perfection.

"That has to be the poorest attempt at a chat up I've ever heard," a deep voice with a thick British accent murmurs in my right ear.

Smirking, I turn slightly to get a better look at the other guy sitting next to me. I do a quick assessment ~ early thirties, attractive face, full head of medium brown hair, nice teeth, not overweight. Yep, I think I found a winner... or a loser, depending on whose point of view you're considering.

"A chat up, eh?" I ask playfully. I lean in close to his ear and whisper, "Something tells me that a 'chat up' isn't what he is really looking for."

He chuckles and shakes his head, then takes a long drink of the amber liquid in his rocks glass. "Something tells me that you're a smart girl."

I smile my most innocent smile and lock my eyes on his. "I'm fucking brilliant," I say with a serious face. He stares at me for a second, almost as if he can't believe I just dropped the F-bomb, and then bursts out laughing.

"Well bloody hell, aren't you the best thing I've met since I've been here?" I beam back at him. He rearranges his body position slightly so that his knee is gently resting against mine before continuing. "I'm Benjamin, by the way."

"Nice to meet you, Benjamin. I'm Chloe," I lie.

And... game over. I win. The victories aren't always this easy, I actually prefer when they put up a little more of a struggle, but tonight I'll take it. Over the next forty minutes, I entertain him by pretending I care about his important marketing job and his growing up in London while sipping on my drink. I laugh when I'm supposed to, touch his arm and leg here and there, and pretend that I don't notice him staring at my boobs. Finally, he asks if I'm interested in sharing a night cap at his place. After explaining that I'm not the kind of girl that goes to a stranger's place, I suggest a hotel room. As his eyes light up and he adjusts his crotch, thinking that he's sealed the deal, the disgust rolls through my body. They are all the same.

Benjamin pays for both of our drinks and we walk out of the bar, hand in hand. Leo is waiting and ushers us into the vehicle. The surprise is evident on Benjamin's face, but he refrains from saying anything. By the look of his clothing and the Hublot timepiece adorning his left wrist, he's no stranger to luxury, but I'm guessing that he wasn't expecting this from me. Once we are both securely in the back seat and on our way to our destination, I twist in my seat and place my hand high up on his thigh.

"Benjamin, would you be interested in playing a little game?" I ask, my voice dripping with sugary sweetness. He first looks down at my hand and then slowly brings his gaze up to my face.

"Absolutely, my pretty little Chloe," he replies with a shit-eating grin. His words make me want to vomit, but instead, I scoot my hand up a bit on his leg and bite my lip suggestively. He leans into me and lightly kisses my exposed neck. "Whatever you want to do, I'm good with," he murmurs against my sensitive skin.

I reach underneath my seat and pull out a piece of heavy black fabric. Crawling onto his lap and straddling his thighs, I gently brush my lips across his before tying the blindfold around his eyes. I feel him tense a little bit as I take away his sight and the excitement begins to bloom inside of me. Next, I retrieve the metal restraints and cuff his wrists together behind his back.

"You're a kinky little thing, aren't you?" I can hear a trace of fear in his voice but the bulge in his pants that continues to grow tells me that he's eager for what he thinks is about to happen.

"You have no idea, Benjamin," I respond in a husky voice. Seeing him so vulnerable, without the ability to see or move his hands, has my body humming. "You won't forget this night for quite some time." I look over my shoulder to get Leo's attention and twirl my finger in the air, indicating that I just want him to drive around. This isn't going to take long; I'm losing interest in this guy before the fun has even started. Briefly, I question what is wrong with me, hoping I'm not growing soft, but then I look down at my dress and I know... I should've worn black. It's my own fault for breaking the rules.

Turning my attention back to him, I lazily begin to unbutton his dress shirt to expose his chest to me, followed by unfastening his belt and dress pants. I skillfully pull his pants and boxers down over his hips until they are around his ankles. His medium-sized cock is standing at complete attention and I can see his pulse racing in his neck. I climb back on his lap, pulling my dress up around my waist and begin to grind my panty-covered pussy on his bare cock. The neckline of the dress pulls down easily along with my bra, so I pop my boobs out and stick them up to his mouth. He needs no words of encouragement; he quickly draws one of my nipples into his mouth and begins sucking forcefully. I increase the speed and pressure of my movements while he devours my breasts; my pussy's growing more and more wet as I anticipate what's about to happen.

Suddenly, I pull my hardened nipple from his mouth and turn around in his lap. My back now to his chest, I roll my hips around so that his jumping cock is nestled in between my ass cheeks and my clit is firmly pressing down on his tight balls. I reach down and slide two of my fingers into my slick opening, rubbing my juices all over my mound. I know he can smell my excitement, and with the way he's writhing around underneath me, I know that he's dying to touch me. He keeps lifting his hips up to press further into me, but each time he does, I stop moving until he relaxes back into the seat.

I continue the torturous treatment for several minutes, bringing myself closer and closer to my release, but never following through. I lift my hand to my breasts - pinching and pulling on my nipples - making them even harder than they were. I catch Leo watching in the rearview mirror and I smile at him, knowing that he's enjoying the show. Nearing the end of my playtime, I dip my fingers inside my hot core once again and lean back onto Benjamin.

"Taste me," I instruct him as I place my fingers on his mouth. Like a starved animal, he opens his mouth and begins sucking and licking my sweet juices off of my hand.

"Fuck, Chloe, you taste even better than I imagined," he growls. "Please, bury my cock inside of that sweet pussy. I'm dying here." I pull my hand from his greedy mouth and evilly laugh as I climb off of his lap. The SUV comes to a gradual stop in an unpopulated alley.

"Funny choice of words, asshole. Unfortunately, you have no idea what dying really feels like, but you and your blue balls are sure to be uncomfortable while hanging out in the cold." The door opens and Leo grabs him by the arms, pulling him out of the car. He's yelling expletives and thrashing around, but he's pretty helpless without the use of his hands and not being able to see. Before I close the door, I call out to him, "I'm sure you've fucked over a female in your life at some point. Consider this payback."

Moments later, we're speeding away from his pitiful ass and on our way to my Central Park apartment. I continue to play with myself the entire drive back, not caring in the least that Leo watches; he always does.

We pull into my parking spot and he escorts me up the elevator and through the front door. Once inside, he undresses me in my lust-hungry state, and then licks me until I cover his face with my sweet cream. He really does the most amazing things with his mouth – lapping, curling, sucking, and nipping until my body quakes violently with relief. Then he carries me to bed and tucks me in, kissing me on my forehead.

"Goodnight, Leo. Thank you for taking care of me," I mumble sleepily.

"Yes ma'am, Miss Kat. I'll see you tomorrow."

And he disappears.

Acknowledgements

A huge thank you to my family for their continued support throughout this entire year as I've embarked on this journey that I never planned on taking, especially my husband and my girls who have had to deal with my hours upon hours of time spent in the cave. They keep a smile on my face and remind me of why I am doing this. I love you all so very much.

To the best betas/ support group a girl could have ~ Trina, Kirsten, Michelle, Shelly, and Jennifer: Thank you for the incredible amount of time and effort that you've put into both this book and my sanity. I couldn't do it without you.

Stephanie: For this incredible idea, Mason is yours forever! Love ya, chica!

Shelly: Thank you for EVERYTHING!!!!

My editor ~ Kayla ("Twinnie"): Thank you, *thank you,* and THANK YOU!

Hang Le: As always, I love it. My Mase and Scarlett are all grown up.

Nicki: I love you, woman.

My bubble of friends ~ you know who you are: Cookie bouquets, cupcakes, chocolates, and wine deliveries... now this is what true friendships are made of.

My mom & Lenora: For everything, always. I love you more than you could ever know.

The bloggers: You ladies are the reason that I'm getting to pursue this dream. Thank you from the bottom of my heart for the time you spend - not only reading, but reviewing and promoting as well.

Kassi Bland Cooper: For fitting me in, for dealing with my crazy, for making it beautiful!!! Thank you!

My baby street team: Huge thanks for pimping me and all of the teasers photos! You ladies are so dear to me.

Erin Noelle is a Texas native, where she lives with her husband and two young daughters. While earning her degree in History at the University of Houston, she rediscovered her love for reading that was first instilled by her grandmother when she was a young child. A lover of happily-ever-afters, both historical and current, Erin is an avid reader of all romance novels. In 2013, she published the Book Boyfriend Series, which included books Metamorphosis, Ambrosia, and Euphoria. Her books have been a part of the USA Today Bestselling list and/ or the Amazon and Barnes & Noble overall Top 100. You can follow her on Facebook @ www.facebook.com/erin.noelle.98, her blog @ www.erinnoelleauthor.com, and on Twitter @authorenoelle.

16862175R00050

Made in the USA
Middletown, DE
23 December 2014